PENGUIN BOOKS

A MAN OF THE PEOPLE

Chinua Achebe (1930–2013) was born in Nigeria. Widely considered to be the father of modern African literature, he is best known for his masterful African Trilogy, consisting of *Things Fall Apart*, *Arrow of God*, and *No Longer at Ease*. The trilogy tells the story of a single Nigerian community over three generations from first colonial contact to urban migration and the breakdown of traditional cultures. He is also the author of *Anthills of the Savannah*, *A Man of the People*, *Girls at War and Other Stories*, *Home and Exile*, *Hopes and Impediments*, *Collected Poems*, *The Education of a British-Protected Child*, *Chike and the River*, and *There Was a Country*. He was the David and Marianna Fisher University Professor and Professor of Africana Studies at Brown University and, for more than fifteen years, was the Charles P. Stevenson Jr. Professor of Languages and Literature at Bard College. Achebe was the recipient of the Nigerian National Merit Award, Nigeria's highest award for intellectual achievement. In 2007, Achebe was awarded the Man Booker International Prize for lifetime achievement.

Books by Chinua Achebe

CHINUA ACHEBE

A Man of the People

PENGUIN BOOKS

PENGUIN BOOKS
An imprint of Penguin Random House LLC
375 Hudson Street
New York, New York 10014
penguin.com

First Anchor Books edition published 1967
Published in Penguin Books 2016

LIBRARY OF CONGRESS CATALOGING-IN-PUBLICATION DATA
Achebe, Chinua.
A man of the people / Chinua Achebe.
p.   cm.
Reprint. Originally published Garden City, N.Y.:
Anchor Books, 1967.
I. Title.
PR9387.9.A3M3   1989   88-22904
823—dc19
ISBN 9780385086165

Printed in the United States of America
50   49   48   47

For J.P. and Chris

A Man of the People

1

No one can deny that Chief the Honourable M. A. Nanga, M.P., was the most approachable politician in the country. Whether you asked in the city or in his home village, Anata, they would tell you he was a man of the people. I have to admit this from the onset or else the story I'm going to tell will make no sense.

That afternoon he was due to address the staff and students of the Anata Grammar School where I was teaching at the time. But as usual in those highly political times the villagers moved in and virtually took over. The Assembly Hall must have carried well over thrice its capacity. Many villagers sat on the floor, right up to the foot of the dais. I took one look and decided it was just as well we had to stay outside—at least for the moment.

Five or six dancing groups were performing at different points in the compound. The popular "Ego Women's Party" wore a new uniform of expensive accra cloth. In spite of the din you could still hear as clear as a bird the high-powered voice of their soloist, whom they admiringly nicknamed "Grammar-phone". Personally I don't care too much for our women's dancing but you just had to listen whenever Grammar-phone sang. She was now praising Micah's handsomeness, which she likened to the perfect, sculpted beauty of a carved eagle, and his popularity which would be the envy of the proverbial traveller-to-distant-places who must not cultivate enmity on his route. Micah was of course Chief the Honourable M. A. Nanga, M.P.

The arrival of the members of the hunters' guild in full regalia caused a great stir. Even Grammar-phone stopped—at least for a while. These people never came out except at the funeral of one of their number, or during some very special and outstanding event. I could not remember when I last saw them. They wielded their loaded guns as though they were playthings. Now and again two of them would meet in warriors' salute and knock the barrel of their guns together from left to right and again from right to left. Mothers grabbed their children and hurriedly dragged them away. Occasionally a hunter would take aim at a distant palm branch and break its mid-rib. The crowd applauded. But there were very few such shots. Most of the hunters reserved their precious powder to greet the Minister's arrival—the price of gunpowder like everything else having doubled again and again in the four years since this government took control.

As I stood in one corner of that vast tumult waiting for the arrival of the Minister I felt intense bitterness welling up in my mouth. Here were silly, ignorant villagers dancing themselves lame and waiting to blow off their gunpowder in honour of one of those who had started the country off down the slopes of inflation. I wished for a miracle, for a voice of thunder, to hush this ridiculous festival and tell the poor contemptible people one or two truths. But of course it would be quite useless. They were not only ignorant but cynical. Tell them that this man had used his position to enrich himself and they would ask you—as my father did—if you thought that a sensible man would spit out the juicy morsel that good fortune placed in his mouth.

I had not always disliked Mr Nanga. Sixteen years or so ago he had been my teacher in standard three and I something like his favourite pupil. I remember him then as a popular, young and handsome teacher, most impressive in his uniform as scoutmaster. There was on one of the walls of the school a painting of a faultlessly handsome scoutmaster wearing an impeccable uniform. I am not sure that the art teacher who painted the picture had Mr Nanga in mind. There was no facial resemblance; still we called it the picture of Mr Nanga. It was enough that they were both handsome and that they were both impressive scoutmasters. This picture stood with arms folded across its chest and its raised right foot resting neatly and lightly on a perfectly cut tree stump. Bright red hibiscus flowers decorated the four corners of the frame; and below were inscribed the memorable words: *Not what I have but what I do is my kingdom.* That was in 1948.

Nanga must have gone into politics soon afterwards and then won a seat in Parliament. (It was easy in those days— before we knew its cash price.) I used to read about him in the papers some years later and even took something like pride in him. At that time I had just entered the University and was very active in the Students' branch of the People's Organization Party. Then in 1960 something disgraceful happened in the Party and I was completely disillusioned.

At that time Mr Nanga was an unknown back-bencher in the governing P.O.P. A general election was imminent. The P.O.P. was riding high in the country and there was no fear of its not being returned. Its opponent, the Progressive Alliance Party, was weak and disorganized.

Then came the slump in the international coffee market. Overnight (or so it seemed to us) the Government had a dangerous financial crisis on its hands. Coffee was the prop of our economy just as coffee farmers were the bulwark of the P.O.P.

The Minister of Finance at the time was a first-rate economist with a Ph.D. in public finance. He presented to the Cabinet a complete plan for dealing with the situation.

The Prime Minister said "No" to the plan. He was not going to risk losing the election by cutting down the price paid to coffee planters at that critical moment; the National Bank should be instructed to print fifteen million pounds. Two-thirds of the Cabinet supported the Minister. The next morning the Prime Minister sacked them and in the evening he broadcast to the nation. He said the dismissed ministers were conspirators and traitors who had teamed up with foreign saboteurs to destroy the new nation.

I remember this broadcast very well. Of course no one knew the truth at that time. The newspapers and the radio carried the Prime Minister's version of the story. We were very indignant. Our Students' Union met in emergency session and passed a vote of confidence in the leader and called for a detention law to deal with the miscreants. The whole country was behind the leader. Protest marches and demonstrations were staged up and down the land.

It was at this point that I first noticed a new, dangerous and sinister note in the universal outcry.

The *Daily Chronicle,* an official organ of the P.O.P., had pointed out in an editorial that the Miscreant Gang, as the dismissed ministers were now called, were all university people and highly educated professional men. (I have preserved a cutting of that editorial.)

> Let us now and for all time extract from our body-politic as a dentist extracts a stinking tooth all those decadent stooges versed in text-book economics and aping the white man's mannerisms and way of speaking. We are proud to be Africans. Our true leaders are not those intoxicated with their Oxford, Cambridge or Harvard degrees but those who speak the language of the people. Away with the damnable and expensive university education which only alienates an African from his rich and ancient culture and puts him above his people. . . .

This cry was taken up on all sides. Other newspapers pointed out that even in Britain where the Miscreant Gang got its "so-called education" a man need not be an economist to be Chancellor of the Exchequer or a doctor to be Minister of Health. What mattered was loyalty to the party.

I was in the public gallery the day the Prime Minister received his overwhelming vote of confidence. And that was the day the truth finally came out; only no one was listening. I remember the grief-stricken figure of the dismissed Minister of Finance as he led his team into the chamber and was loudly booed by members and the public. That week his car had been destroyed by angry mobs and his house stoned. Another dismissed minister had been pulled out of his car, beaten insensible, and dragged along the road for fifty yards, then tied hand and foot, gagged and left by the roadside. He was still in the orthopaedic hospital when the house met.

That was my first—and last—visit to Parliament. It was also the only time I had set eyes on Mr Nanga again since he taught me in 1948.

The Prime Minister spoke for three hours and his every other word was applauded. He was called the Tiger, the Lion, the One and Only, the Sky, the Ocean and many other names of praise. He said that the Miscreant Gang had been caught "red-handed in their nefarious plot to overthrow the Government of the people by the people and for the people with the help of enemies abroad".

"They deserve to be hanged," shouted Mr Nanga from the back benches. This interruption was so loud and clear that it appeared later under his own name in the Hansard. Throughout the session he led the pack of back-bench hounds straining their leash to get at their victims. If any one had cared to sum up Mr Nanga's interruptions they would have made a good hour's continuous yelp. Perspiration poured down his face as he sprang up to interrupt or sat back to share in the derisive laughter of the hungry hyena.

When the Prime Minister said that he had been stabbed in the back by the very ingrates he had pulled out of oblivion some members were in tears.

"They have bitten the finger with which their mother fed them," said Mr Nanga. This too was entered in the Hansard, a copy of which I have before me. It is impossible, however, to convey in cold print the electric atmosphere of that day.

I cannot now recall exactly what my feelings were at that point. I suppose I thought the whole performance rather peculiar. You must remember that at that point no one had any reason to think there might be another side to the story. The Prime Minister was still talking. Then he made the now famous (or infamous) solemn declaration: "From today we must watch and guard our hard-won freedom jealously. Never again must we entrust our destiny and the destiny of Africa to the hybrid class of Western-educated and snobbish intellectuals who will not hesitate to sell their mothers for a mess of pottage. . . ."

Mr Nanga pronounced the death sentence at least twice more but this was not recorded, no doubt because his voice was lost in the general commotion.

I remember the figure of Dr Makinde the ex-Minister of Finance as he got up to speak—tall, calm, sorrowful and superior. I strained my ears to catch his words. The entire house, including the Prime Minister tried to shout him down. It was a most unedifying spectacle. The Speaker broke his mallet ostensibly trying to maintain order, but you could see he was enjoying the commotion. The public gallery yelled down its abuses. "Traitor", "Coward", "Doctor of Fork your Mother". This last was contributed from the gallery by the editor of the *Daily Chronicle,* who sat close to me. Encouraged, no doubt, by the volume of laughter this piece of witticism had earned him in the gallery he proceeded the next morning to print it in his paper. The spelling is his.

Although Dr Makinde read his speech, which was clearly prepared, the Hansard later carried a garbled version which made no sense at all. It said not a word about the plan to mint fifteen million pounds—which was perhaps to be expected— but why put into Dr Makinde's mouth words that he could not have spoken? In short the Hansard boys wrote a completely new speech suitable to the boastful villain the ex-minister had become. For instance they made him say he was "a brilliant economist whose reputation was universally acclaimed in Europe". When I read this I was in tears—and I don't cry all that easily.

The reason I have gone into that shameful episode in such detail is to establish the fact that I had no reason to be enthusiastic about Chief the Honourable M. A. Nanga who, seeing the empty ministerial seats, had yapped and snarled so shamelessly for the meaty prize.

The Proprietor and Principal of the school was a thin, wiry fellow called Jonathan Nwege. He was very active in politics at the local council level and was always grumbling because his services to the P.O.P. had not been rewarded with the usual prize-appointment to some public corporation or other. But though disgruntled he had not despaired, as witness his elaborate arrangements for the present reception. Perhaps he was hoping for something in the proposed new corporation which would take over the disposal of all government unserviceable property (like old mattresses, chairs, electric fans, disused typewriters and other junk) which at present was auctioned by civil servants. I hope he gets appointed. It would have the merit of removing him from the school now and again.

He insisted that the students should mount a guard of honour stretching from the main road to the school door. And the teachers too were to stand in a line at the end of the student queue, to be introduced. Mr Nwege who regularly read such literature as "Toasts—How to Propose Them" was very meticulous about this kind of thing. I had objected vehemently to this standing like school children at our staff meeting, thinking to rouse the other teachers. But the teachers in that school were all dead from the neck up. My friend and colleague Andrew Kadibe found it impossible to side with me because he and the Minister came from the same village. Primitive loyalty, I call it.

As soon as the Minister's Cadillac arrived at the head of a long motorcade the hunters dashed this way and that and let off their last shots, throwing their guns about with frightening freedom. The dancers capered and stamped, filling the dry-season air with dust. Not even Grammar-phone's voice could now be heard over the tumult. The Minister stepped out wearing damask and gold chains and acknowledging cheers with his ever-present fan of animal skin which they said fanned away all evil designs and shafts of malevolence thrown at him by the wicked.

The man was still as handsome and youthful-looking as ever—there was no doubt about that. The Proprietor was now introducing him to the teachers beginning with the Senior Tutor at the head of the line. Although I had not had time to scrutinize the Senior Tutor's person I had no doubt he had traces of snuff as usual in his nostrils. The Minister had a jovial word for everyone. You could never think—looking at him now—that his smile was anything but genuine. It seemed bloody-minded to be sceptical. Now it was my turn. I held out my hand somewhat stiffly. I did not have the slightest fear that he might remember me and had no intention of reminding him.

Our hands met. I looked him straight in the face. The smile slowly creased up into lines of thought. He waved his left hand impatiently to silence the loquacious Proprietor who had begun the parrot formula he had repeated at least fifteen times so far: "I have the honour, sir, to introduce . . ."

"That's right," said the Minister not to anyone in particular, but to some mechanism of memory inside his head. "You are Odili."

"Yes, sir." Before the words were out of my mouth he had thrown his arms round me smothering me in his voluminous damask. "You have a wonderful memory," I said. "It's at least fifteen years . . ." He had now partly released me although his left hand was resting on my shoulder. He turned slightly to the Proprietor and announced proudly:

"I taught him in . . ."

"Standard three," I said.

"That's right," he shouted. If he had just found his long-lost son he could not have been more excited.

"He is one of the pillars of this school," said the Proprietor, catching the infection and saying the first good word about me since I had joined his school.

"Odili, the great," said the Minister boyishly, and still out of breath. "Where have you been all this time?"

I told him I had been to the University, and had been teaching for the last eighteen months.

"Good boy!" he said. "I knew he would go to a university. I used to tell the other boys in my class that Odili will one day be a great man and they will be answering him sir, sir. Why did you not tell me when you left the University? That's very bad of you, you know."

"Well," I said happily—I'm ashamed to admit—"I know how busy a minister . . ."

"Busy? Nonsense. Don't you know that minister means servant? Busy or no busy he must see his master."

Everybody around applauded and laughed. He slapped me again on the back and said I must not fail to see him at the end of the reception.

"If you fail I will send my orderly to arrest you."

I became a hero in the eyes of the crowd. I was dazed. Everything around me became suddenly unreal; the voices receded to a vague border zone. I knew I ought to be angry with myself but I wasn't. I found myself wondering whether—perhaps—I had been applying to politics stringent standards that didn't belong to it. When I came back to the immediate present I heard the Minister saying to another teacher:

"That is very good. Sometimes I used to regret ever leaving the teaching field. Although I am a minister today I can swear to God that I am not as happy as when I was a teacher."

My memory is naturally good. That day it was perfect. I don't know how it happened, but I can recall every word the Minister said on that occasion. I can repeat the entire speech he made later.

"True to God who made me," he insisted. "I used to regret it. Teaching is a very noble profession."

At this point everybody just collapsed with laughter not least of all the Honourable Minister himself, nor me, for that matter. The man's assurance was simply unbelievable. Only he could make such a risky joke—or whatever he thought he was making—at that time, when teachers all over the country

were in an ugly, rebellious mood. When the laughter died
down, he put on a more serious face and confided to us: "You
can rest assured that those of us in the Cabinet who were once
teachers are in full sympathy with you."

"Once a teacher always a teacher," said the Senior Tutor,
adjusting the sleeves of his faded "bottom-box" robes.

"Hear! hear!" I said. I like to think that I meant it to be
sarcastic. The man's charisma had to be felt to be believed. If I
were superstitious I would say he had made a really potent
charm of the variety called "sweet face".

Changing the subject slightly, the Minister said, "Only
teachers can make this excellent arrangement." Then turning
to the newspaper correspondent in his party he said, "It is a
mammoth crowd."

The journalist whipped out his note-book and began to
write.

"It is an unprecedented crowd in the annals of Anata," said
Mr Nwege.

"James, did you hear that?" the Minister asked the journalist.

"No, sir, what is it?"

"This gentleman says it is the most unprecedented crowd
in the annals of Anata," I said. This time I clearly meant my
tongue to be in my cheek.

"What is the gentleman's name?"

Mr Nwege called his name and spelled it and gave his full
title of "Principal and Proprietor of Anata Grammar School".
Then he turned to the Minister in an effort to pin-point responsibility for the big crowds.

"I had to visit every section of the village personally to tell
them of your—I mean to say of the Minister's—visit."

We had now entered the Assembly Hall and the Minister and
his party were conducted to their seats on the dais. The crowd
raised a deafening shout of welcome. He waved his fan to the
different parts of the hall. Then he turned to Mr Nwege and said:

"Thank you very much, thank you, sir."

A huge, tough-looking member of the Minister's entourage who stood with us at the back of the dais raised his voice and said:

"You see wetin I de talk. How many minister fit hanswer *sir* to any Tom, Dick and Harry wey senior them for age? I hask you how many?"

Everyone at the dais agreed that the Minister was quite exceptional in this respect—a man of high position who still gave age the respect due to it. No doubt it was a measure of my changed—or shall we say changing?—attitude to the Minister that I found myself feeling a little embarrassed on his account for these fulsome praises flung at his face.

"Minister or no minister," he said, "a man who is my senior must still be my senior. Other ministers and other people may do otherwise but my motto is: *Do the right and shame the Devil.*"

Somehow I found myself admiring the man for his lack of modesty. For what is modesty but inverted pride? We all think we are first-class people. Modesty forbids us from saying so ourselves though, presumably, not from wanting to hear it from others. Perhaps it was their impatience with this kind of hypocrisy that made men like Nanga successful politicians while starry-eyed idealists strove vaingloriously to bring into politics niceties and delicate refinements that belonged elsewhere.

While I thought about all this—perhaps not in these exact terms—the fulsome praises flowed all around the dais.

Mr Nwege took the opportunity to mount his old hobbyhorse. The Minister's excellent behaviour, he said, was due to the sound education he had received when education *was* education.

"Yes," said the Minister, "I used to tell them that standard six in those days is more than Cambridge today."

"Cambridge?" asked Mr Nwege who, like the Minister, had the good old standard six. "Cambridge? Who dash frog coat? You mean it is equal to B.A. today—if not more."

"With due apologies," said the Minister turning in my direction.

"Not at all, sir," I replied with equal good humour. "I am

applying for a post-graduate scholarship to bring myself up to
Mr Nwege's expectation."

I remember that at that point the beautiful girl in the
Minister's party turned round on her chair to look at me. My
eyes met hers and she quickly turned round again. I think the
Minister noticed it.

"My private secretary has B.A. from Oxford," he said.
"He should have come with me on this tour but I had some
office work for him to do. By the way, Odili, I think you are
wasting your talent here. I want you to come to the capital
and take up a strategic post in the civil service. We shouldn't
leave everything to the highland tribes. My secretary is from
there; our people must press for their fair share of the national cake."

The hackneyed phrase "national cake" was getting to some
of us for the first time, and so it was greeted with applause.

"Owner of book!" cried one admirer, assigning in those
three brief words the ownership of the white man's language to
the Honourable Minister, who turned round and beamed on the
speaker.

That was when my friend Andrew Kadibe committed the
unpardonable indiscretion of calling the Minister the nickname he had worn as a teacher: "M.A. Minus Opportunity." It
was particularly bad because Andrew and the Minister were
from the same village.

The look he gave Andrew then reminded me of that other
Nanga who had led the pack of hounds four years ago.

"Sorry, sir," said Andrew pitiably.

"Sorry for what?" snarled the Minister.

"Don't mind the *stupid* boy, sir," said Mr Nwege, greatly
upset. "This is what we were saying before."

"I think we better begin," said the Minister, still
frowning.

Although Mr Nwege had begun by saying that the distin-
guished guest needed no introduction he had gone on all the
same to talk for well over twenty minutes—largely in praise

of himself and all he had done for the Party in Anata "and environs".

The crowd became steadily more restive especially when they noticed that the Minister was looking at his watch. Loud grumbles began to reach the dais from the audience. Then clear voices telling Nwege to sit down and let the man they came to hear talk. Nwege ignored all these warning signs—a more insensitive man you never saw. Finally one of the tough young men of the village stood up ten feet or so away and shouted:

"It is enough or I shall push you down and take three pence."

This did the trick. The laughter that went up must have been heard a mile away. Mr Nwege's concluding remarks were completely lost. In fact it was not until the Minister rose to his feet that the laughter stopped.

The story had it that many years ago when Mr Nwege was a poor, hungry elementary school teacher—that is before he built his own grammar school and became rich but apparently still hungry—he had an old rickety bicycle of the kind the villagers gave the onomatopoeic name of *anikilija*. Needless to say the brakes were very faulty. One day as he was cascading down a steep slope that led to a narrow bridge at the bottom of the hill he saw a lorry—an unusual phenomenon in those days—coming down the opposite slope. It looked like a head-on meeting on the bridge. In his extremity Mr Nwege had raised his voice and cried to passing pedestrians: "In the name of God push me down!" Apparently nobody did, and so he added an inducement: "Push me down and my three pence is yours!" From that day "Push me down and take my three pence" became a popular Anata joke.

The Minister's speech sounded spontaneous and was most effective. There was no election at hand, he said, amid laughter. He had not come to beg for their votes; it was just "a family reunion—pure and simple". He would have preferred not to speak to his own kinsmen in English which was after all a foreign language, but he had learned from experience that speeches made in vernacular were liable to be distorted and misquoted in the press. Also there were some strangers in that audience who did not speak our own tongue and he did not wish to exclude them. They were all citizens of our great country whether they came from the highlands or the lowlands, etc. etc.

The stranger he had in mind I think was Mrs Eleanor John, an influential party woman from the coast who had come in the Minister's party. She was heavily painted and perfumed and although no longer young seemed more than able to hold her own, if it came to that. She sat on the Minister's left, smoking and fanning herself. Next to her sat the beautiful young girl I have talked about. I didn't catch the two of them exchanging any words or even looks. I wondered what such a girl was doing in that tough crowd; it looked as though they had stopped by some convent on their way and offered to give her a lift to the next one.

At the end of his speech the Minister and his party were invited to the Proprietor's Lodge—as Mr Nwege called his square, cement-block house. Outside, the dancers had all come alive again and the hunters—their last powder gone—were tamely waiting for the promised palm-wine. The Minister danced a few dignified steps to the music of each group and stuck red pound notes on the perspiring faces of the best dancers. To one group alone he gave away five pounds.

The same man who had drawn our attention to the Minister's humility was now pointing out yet another quality. I looked at him closely for the first time and noticed that he had one bad eye—what we call a cowrie-shell eye.

"You see how e de do as if to say money be san-san," he was saying. "People wey de jealous the money gorment de pay Minister no sabi say no be him one de chop am. Na so so troway."

Later on in the Proprietor's Lodge I said to the Minister: "You must have spent a fortune today."

He smiled at the glass of cold beer in his hand and said:

"You call this spend? You never see some thing, my brother. I no de keep anini for myself, na so so troway. If some person come to you and say 'I wan' make you Minister' make you run like blazes comot. Na true word I tell you. To God who made me." He showed the tip of his tongue to the sky to confirm the oath. "Minister de sweet for eye but too much katakata de for inside. Believe me yours sincerely."

"Big man, big palaver," said the one-eyed man.

It was left to Josiah, owner of a nearby shop-and-bar to sound a discordant, if jovial, note.

"Me one," he said, "I no kuku mind the katakata wey de for inside. Make you put Minister money for my hand and all the wahala on top. I no mind at all."

Everyone laughed. Then Mrs John said:

"No be so, my frien'. When you done experience rich man's trouble you no fit talk like that again. My people get one proverb: they say that when poor man done see with his own eye how to make big man e go beg make e carry him poverty de go je-je."

They said this woman was a very close friend of the Minister's, and her proprietary air would seem to confirm it and the fact that she had come all the way from Pokoma, three hundred and fifty miles away. I knew of her from the newspapers; she was a member of the Library Commission, one of the statutory boards within the Minister's portfolio. Her massive coral beads were worth hundreds of pounds according to the whisper circulating in the room while she talked. She was the "merchant princess" *par excellence*. Poor beginning—an orphan, I believe—no school education, plenty of good looks and an iron determination, both of which she put to good account; beginning as a street hawker, rising to a small trader, and then to a big one. At present, they said, she presided over the entire trade in imported second-hand clothing worth hundreds of thousands.

I edged quietly towards the journalist who seemed to know everyone in the party and whispered in his ear: "Who is the young lady?"

"Ah," he said, leaving his mouth wide open for a while as a danger signal. "Make you no go near am-o. My hand no de for inside."

I told him I wasn't going near am-o; I merely asked who she was.

"The Minister no de introduce-am to anybody. So I think say na im girl-friend, or im cousin." Then he confided: "I done lookam, lookam, lookam sotay I tire. I no go tell you lie girls for this una part sabi fine-o. God Almighty!"

I had also noticed that the Minister had skipped her when he had introduced his party to the teachers.

I know it sounds silly, but I began to wonder what had happened to the Mrs Nanga of the scoutmastering days. They were newly married then. I remembered her particularly because she was one of the very first women I knew to wear a white, ladies' helmet which in our ignorance we called *helment* and which was in those days the very acme of sophistication.

2

A common saying in the country after Independence was that it didn't matter *what* you knew but *who* you knew. And, believe me, it was no idle talk. For a person like me who simply couldn't stoop to lick any Big Man's boots it created a big problem. In fact one reason why I took this teaching job in a bush, private school instead of a smart civil service job in the city with car, free housing, etc., was to give myself a certain amount of autonomy. So when I told the Minister that I had applied for a scholarship to do a post-graduate Certificate of Education in London it did not even cross my mind to enlist his help. I think it is important to stress this point. I had had scholarships both to the secondary school and to the University without any godfather's help but purely on my own merit. And in any case it wasn't too important whether I did the post-graduate course or not. As far as I was concerned the important thing was going to be the opportunity of visiting

Europe which in itself must be a big education. My friend Andrew Kadibe, who did the same course the previous year, seemed to have got a big kick out of it. I don't mean the white girls—you can have those out here nowadays—but quite small things. I remember him saying for instance that the greatest delight of his entire visit to Britain was when, for the first time in his twenty-seven years, a white man—a taxi-driver I think—carried his suitcase and said "Sir" to him. He was so thrilled he tipped the man ten shillings. We laughed a lot about it but I could so easily see it happen.

But much as I wanted to go to Europe I wasn't going to sell my soul for it or beg anyone to help me. It was the Minister himself who came back to the post-graduate question at the end of his reception without any prompting whatever from me. (As a matter of fact I tried hard to avoid catching his attention again.) And the proposals he made didn't seem to me to be offensive in any way. He invited me to come and spend my holidays with him in the capital and while I was there he would try and find out from his Cabinet colleague, the Minister of Overseas Training, whether there was anything doing.

"If you come as soon as you close," he said, "you can stay in my guest-room with everything complete—bedroom, parlour, bathroom, latrine, everything—self-contained. You can live by yourself and do *anything* you like there, it's all yours."

"Make you no min' am, sha-a," said Mrs John to me. "I kin see say you na good boy. Make you no gree am spoil you. Me I no de for dis bed-room and bath-room business-o. As you see dis man so, na wicked soul. If he tell you stand make you run."

Everybody laughed.

"Eleanor, why you wan disgrace me and spoil my name so for public for nothing sake. Wetin I do you? Everybody here sabi say me na good Christian. No be so, James?"

"Ah, na so, sir," replied the journalist happily.

In spite of all this joking the Minister's invitation was serious and firm. He said it was important I came at once as he was planning to go to the United States in about two months.

"They are going to give me doctorate degree," he announced proudly. "Doctor of Laws, LL.D."

"That's great," I said. "Congratulations."

"Thank you, my brother."

"So the Minister will become 'Chief the Honourable Doctor M. A. Nanga'," intoned the journalist, a whole second ahead of my own thoughts on the matter. We all cheered the impressive address and its future owner.

"You no see say the title fit my name *pem*," said the Minister with boyish excitement, and we all said yes it suited him perfectly.

"But the man wey I like him name pass na 'Chief the Honourable Alhaji Doctor Mongo Sego, M.P.'," said the Minister somewhat wistfully.

"Him own good too," admitted the incomparable journalist, "but e no pass your own, sir: 'Chief the Honourable Dr M. A. Nanga, M.P., LL.D.' Na waa! Nothing fit passam."

"What about 'Chief Dr Mrs'?" I threw in mischievously.

"That one no sweet for mouth," said the Minister. "E no catch."

"Wetin wrong with am?" asked Mrs John. "Because na woman get am e no go sweet for mouth. I done talk say na only for election time woman de get equality for dis our country."

"No be so, madam," said the journalist. "You no see how the title rough like sand-paper for mouth: 'Dr Chief Mrs'. E no catch at all."

Before the Minister left he made sure I took down his residential address in the capital. I felt Mr Nwege's malevolent eyes boring into me as I wrote it down. And hardly were the farewells out of his mouth before he turned to me and asked sneeringly if I was still of the opinion that it was unnecessary to be introduced to the Minister.

"What I objected to was standing in a line like school children," I said, somewhat embarrassed. "In any case I didn't need to be introduced. We knew each other already."

"You can thank your stars that I am not a wicked man," he

continued as though I had said nothing, "otherwise I would have told him. . . ."

"Why don't you run after him now?" I asked. "He cannot have gone very far." With that I walked away from the obsequious old fool.

But when I came to think of the events of the day I had to admit that Mr Nwege had not had fair returns for all his trouble. I don't think the Minister gave him as much as a second to raise any of his own problems. And it was uncharitable I thought for him to have joined in as loudly as he had done in the "push me down" laughter. For the sake of appearances at least he should have kept a straight face. It was clear the great man did not easily forgive those who took up part of his time to make their own speeches. He ostentatiously ignored Mr Nwege for the rest of the day. Poor man! He had probably lost the chance of getting on that new corporation for the disposal of dilapidated government wares with which he was no doubt hoping to replace the even more worn-out equipment in his school. So although it was unreasonable for him to have turned his anger on me there was no doubt he had cause to be angry.

Actually his teachers had let him down badly that afternoon. Apart from myself there was that "M.A. minus opportunity" incident which for some obscure reason seemed to have annoyed the Minister even more than Mr Nwege's long speech. At least he contained the latter annoyance with laughter. And to crown Mr Nwege's discomfitures his Senior Tutor, a man in his sixties, had sallied out of the Lodge with one bottle of beer under each armpit—to the amusement of everyone except Mr Nwege who had clearly not gone out of his way to buy beer at its present impossible price for members of his staff to take home. The Senior Tutor, by the way, was a jolly old rogue who could get away with anything—if need be by playing the buffoon. He was a great frequenter of Josiah's bar across the road. He had a fine sense of humour—like when he asked why so many young people travelled to Britain to be called to the Bar when he could call them all to Josiah's bar.

I was lighting my Tilley lamp later that evening when someone knocked on my door.

"Come in if you are good-looking," I said.

"Is Odili in?" asked an unnatural, high-pitched voice.

"Come in, fool," I said.

It was a silly joke Andrew and I never tired of playing on each other. The idea was to sound like a girl and so send the other's blood pressure up.

"How the go de go?" I asked.

"Bo, son of man done tire."

"Did you find out about that girl?" I asked.

"Why na so so girl, girl, girl, girl been full your mouth. Wetin? So person no fit talk any serious talk with you. I never see."

"O.K., Mr Gentleman," I said, pumping the lamp. "Any person wey first mention about girl again for this room make him tongue cut. How is the weather?" He laughed.

At that point my house-boy, a fifteen-year-old rogue called Peter, came in to ask what he should cook for supper.

"You no hear the news for three o'clock?" I asked, feigning great seriousness.

"Sir?"

"Government done pass new law say na only two times a day person go de chop now. For morning and for afternoon. Finish."

He laughed.

"That is next to impossibility," he said. Peter liked his words long. He had his standard six certificate which two or three years before could have got him a job as a messenger in an office or even a teacher in an elementary school. But today there simply aren't any jobs for his kind of person any more and he was lucky to be a sort of housekeeper to me for one pound a month, including, of course, free board and lodging. He spent most of his spare time reading, although his favourite literature is of a very dubious kind. I once found him reading a strange book he had just received from India. I think it was called *How to Solve the Fair Sex* and had cost him no less than ten shillings excluding postage from New Delhi. I had roundly rebuked him.

I couldn't think what to eat. So I told him to go and roast me some yams.

"Roast yams at night?" screamed Andrew. "If you knock at my door in the middle of the night I shan't wake up."

This was a crude reference to the night I had a violent stomach-ache after eating half a dozen roasted corn. I had been so scared I had gone and called Andrew up to take me to hospital in his ancient car.

"What do you suggest I eat then?" I asked him.

"Am I your wife? Don't you see all the girls waiting for husbands?"

"Don't you fear. I have my eyes on one *right* now."

"True? Give me tori. Who is she? What about the poem?"

"The same," I said, and we recited together a poem one of our acquaintances had composed for his wedding invitation card:

> *"It's time to spread the news abroad*
> *That we are well prepared*
> *To tie ourselves with silvery cord*
> *Of sweet conjugal bond."*

"Look at this small pickin," said Andrew in pretended anger to Peter who had joined our laughter. "How dare you laugh with your elders?"

"Sorry, sir," said Peter, frowning comically.

"What do you think I should eat, Peter?" I asked.

"Anything master talk. Like Jollof rice, sir."

I knew. Whenever you allowed him a say in this matter he invariably came up with Jollof rice—his favourite dish.

"O.K.," I said. "One cup of rice—not one and a half; not one and a quarter."

"Yes, sir," he said, and went away happily. I knew he would cook at least two cups.

"Who is she?" I said.

"Who?"

"The girl with the Minister."

"His girl-friend."

"I see."

"Actually it's more than that. He is planning to marry her according to native law and custom. Apparently his missus is too 'bush' for his present position so he wants a bright new 'parlour-wife' to play hostess at his parties."

"Too bad. Who told you all this?"

"Somebody."

"Too bad. Without knowing anything whatever about that girl I feel she deserves to be somebody's first wife—not an old man's mistress. Anyway it's none of my business."

"He sent her to a Women's Training College," said Andrew. "So he has been planning it for a few years at least. I feel sorry for her; that man has no conscience."

I said nothing.

"Imagine such a beautiful thing wasting herself on such an empty-headed ass. I so enjoyed wounding his pride! Did you see how wild he looked?"

"Yes," I said, "you hit him hard." Actually I was amused how Andrew was desperately trying to convince himself—and me—that he had gone to the reception with the avowed intention to deflate his empty-headed *kontriman*. He seemed to be forgetting in a hurry that he had earlier refused to support me at the staff meeting when I had objected to Mr Nwege's stupid plans.

"Just think of such a cultureless man going abroad and calling himself Minister of Culture. Ridiculous. This is why the outside world laughs at us."

"That is true," I said, "but the outside world isn't all that important, is it? In any case people like Chief Nanga don't care two hoots about the outside world. He is concerned with the inside world, with how to retain his hold on his constituency and there he is adept, you must admit. Anyway, as he told us today, Churchill never passed his School Certificate."

"I see the offer of free lodging is already having its effect."

I began to laugh and Andrew joined in. You could tell at a

glance that he knew me in a way that Mr Nwege didn't. It was one thing to tease me for accepting the Minister's offer of accommodation, but I just didn't want anybody to think that Odili Samalu was capable of stooping to obtain a scholarship in any underhand way. In the words of my boy, Peter, it was "next to impossibility".

Andrew knew of course that I had long been planning to go to the capital and he knew about Elsie.

Well, Elsie! Where does one begin to write about her? The difficulty in writing this kind of story is that the writer is armed with all kinds of hindsight which he didn't have when the original events were happening. When he introduces a character like Elsie for instance, he already has at the back of his mind a total picture of her; her entrance, her act and her exit. And this tends to colour even the first words he writes. I can only hope that being aware of this danger I have successfully kept it at bay. As far as is humanly possible I shall try not to jump ahead of my story.

Elsie was, and for that matter still is, the only girl I met and slept with the same day—in fact within an hour. I know that faster records do exist and am not entering this one for that purpose, nor am I trying to prejudice anyone against Elsie. I only put it down because that was the way it happened. It was during my last term at the University and, having as usual put off my revision to the last moment, I was having a rough time. But one evening there was a party organized by the Students' Christian Movement and I decided in spite of my arrears of work to attend and give my brain time to cool off. I am not usually lucky, but that evening I was. I saw Elsie standing in a group with other student nurses and made straight for her. She turned out to be a most vivacious girl newly come to the nursing School. We danced twice, then I suggested we take a walk away from the noisy highlife band and she readily agreed. If I had been left to my own devices nothing might have happened that day. But, no doubt without meaning to, Elsie took a hand in the matter. She said she was thirsty and I took her to my rooms for a drink of water.

She was one of those girls who send out loud cries in the

heat of the thing. It happened again each time. But that first day it was rather funny because she kept calling: "Ralph darling." I remember wondering why Ralph. It was not until weeks later that I got to know that she was engaged to some daft fellow called Ralph, a medical student in Edinburgh. The funny part of it was that my next-door neighbour—an English Honours student and easily the most ruthless and unprincipled womanizer in the entire university campus—changed to calling me Ralph from that day. He was known to most students by his nickname, Irre, which was short for Irresponsible. His most celebrated conquest was a female undergraduate who had seemed so inaccessible that boys called her Unbreakable. Irre became interested in her and promised his friends to break her one day soon. Then one afternoon we saw her enter his rooms. Our hall began to buzz with excitement as word went round, and we stood in little groups all along the corridor, waiting. Half an hour or so later Irre came out glistening with sweat, closed the door quietly behind him and then held up a condom bloated with his disgusting seed. That was Irre for you—a real monster. I suppose I was somehow flattered by the notice a man of such prowess had taken of Elsie's cry. When I confided to him later that Ralph was the name of the girl's proper boy-friend he promptly changed to calling me Assistant Ralph or, if Elsie was around, simply A.R.

Despite this rather precipitous beginning Elsie and I became very good and steady friends. I can't pretend that I ever thought of marriage, but I must admit I did begin to feel a little jealous any time I found her reading and rereading a blue British air-letter with the red Queen and Houses of Parliament stamped on its back. Elsie was such a beautiful, happy girl and she made no demands whatever.

When I left the University she was heart-broken and so was I for that matter. We exchanged letters every week or two weeks at the most. I remember during the postal strike of 1963 when I didn't hear from her for over a month I nearly kicked the bucket, as my boy, Peter, would have said.

Now she was working in a hospital about twelve miles

outside Bori and so we arranged that I should spend my next holidays in the capital and take the bus to her hospital every so often while she would be able to spend her days off in the city. That was why the Minister's offer couldn't have come at a more opportune moment. I had of course one or two bachelor friends in the capital who would have had no difficulty in putting me up. But they weren't likely to provide a guest-room with all amenities.

For days after the Minister's visit I was still trying to puzzle out why he had seemed so offended by his old nickname—"M.A. Minus Opportunity". I don't know why I should have been so preoccupied with such unimportant trash. But it often happens to me like that: I get hold of some pretty inane thought or a cheap tune I would ordinarily be ashamed to be caught whistling, like that radio jingle advertising an intestinal worm expeller, and I get stuck with it.

When I first knew Mr Nanga in 1948 he had seemed quite happy with his nickname. I suspect he had in fact invented it himself. Certainly he enjoyed it. His name being M. A. Nanga, his fellow teachers called him simply and fondly "M.A."; he answered "Minus Opportunity", which he didn't have to do unless he liked it. Why then the present angry reaction? I finally decided that it stemmed from the same general anti-intellectual feeling in the country. In 1948 Mr Nanga could admit, albeit lightheartedly, to a certain secret yearning for higher education; in 1964 he was valiantly proving that a man like him was better without it. Of course he had not altogether persuaded himself, or else he would not have shown such excitement over the LL.D. arranged for him from some small, back-street college.

3

Before making the long journey to the capital, I thought I should first pay a short visit to my home village, Urua, about fifteen miles from Anata. I wanted to see my father about one or two matters but more especially I wanted to take my boy, Peter, to his parents for the holidays as I had promised to do before they let me have him.

Peter was naturally very excited about going home after nearly twelve months, during which he had become a wage-earner. At first I found it amusing when he went over to Josiah's shop across the road and bought a rayon head-tie for his mother and a head of tobacco for his father. But as I thought more about it I realized how those touching gestures by a mere boy, whom I paid twenty shillings a month, showed up my own quite different circumstances. And I felt envious. I had no mother to buy head-ties for, and although I had a father, giving things to him was like pouring a little water into a dried-up well.

My mother had been his second wife, but she had died in her first childbirth. This meant in the minds of my people that I was an unlucky child, if not a downright wicked and evil one. Not that my father ever said so openly. To begin with he had too many other wives and children to take any special notice of me. But I was always a very sensitive child and knew from quite early in my life that there was something wrong with my affairs. My father's first wife, whom we all call Mama, brought me up like one of her own children; still I sensed there was something missing. One day at play another child with whom I had fallen out called me "Bad child that crunched his mother's skull". That was it.

I am not saying that I had an unhappy or a lonely child-hood. There were too many of us in the family for anyone to think of loneliness or unhappiness. And I must say this for my father that he never tolerated any of his wives drawing a line no matter how thin between her own children and those of others. We had only one Mama. The other two wives (at the time—there are more now) were called Mother by their chil-dren, or so and so's mother by the rest.

Of course as soon as I grew old enough to understand a few simple proverbs I realized that I should have died and let my mother live. Whenever my people go to console a woman whose baby has died at birth or soon after, they always tell her to dry her eyes because it is better the water is spilled than the pot broken. The idea being that a sound pot can always return to the stream.

My father was a District Interpreter. In those days when no one understood as much as "come" in the white man's lan-guage, the District Officer was like the Supreme Deity, and the Interpreter the principal minor god who carried prayers and sacrifice to Him. Every sensible supplicant knew that the lesser god must first be wooed and put in a sweet frame of mind before he could undertake to intercede with the Owner of the Sky.

So Interpreters in those days were powerful, very rich, widely known and hated. Wherever the D.O.'s power was felt

—and that meant everywhere—the Interpreter's name was held in fear and trembling.

We grew up knowing that the world was full of enemies. Our father had protective medicine located at crucial points in our house and compound. One, I remember, hung over the main entrance; but the biggest was in a gourd in a corner of his bedroom. No child went alone into that room which was virtually always under lock and key anyway. We were told that such and such homes were never to be entered; and those people were pointed out to us from whom we must not accept food.

But we also had many friends. There were all those people who brought my father gifts of yams, pots of palm-wine or bottles of European drink, goats, sheep, chicken. Or those who brought their children to live with us as house-boys or their brides-to-be for training in modern housekeeping. In spite of the enormous size of our family there was always meat in the house. At one time, I remember, my father used to slaughter a goat every Saturday, which was more than most families did in two years, and this sign of wealth naturally exposed us to their jealousy and malevolence.

But it was not until many years later that I caught one fleeting, terrifying glimpse of just how hated an Interpreter could be. I was in secondary school then and it was our half-term holiday. As my home village was too far away and I didn't want to spend the holiday in school I decided to go with one of my friends to his home which was four or five miles away. His parents were very happy to see us and his mother at once went to boil some yams for us.

After we had eaten, the father who had gone out to buy himself some snuff came hurrying back. To my surprise he asked his son what he said my name was again.

"Odili Samalu."

"Of what town?"

There was anxiety, an uneasy tension in his voice. I was afraid.

"Urua, sir," I said.

"I see," he said coldly. "Who is your father?"

"Hezekiah Samalu," I said and then added quickly, "a retired District Interpreter." It was better, I thought, to come out with it all at once and end the prolonged interrogation.

"Then you cannot stay in my house," he said with that evenness of tone which our people expect a man of substance to use in moments of great crisis when lesser men and women would make loud, empty noises.

"Why, Papa, what has he done?" asked my friend in alarm.

"I have said it. . . . I don't blame you, my son, or you either, because no one has told you. But know it from today that no son of Hezekiah Samalu's shelters under my roof." He looked outside. "There is still light and time for you to get back to the school."

I don't think I shall ever know just in what way my father had wronged that man. A few weeks later, during the next holidays I tried to find out, but all my father did was to rave at me for wandering like a homeless tramp when I should be working at the books he sent me to school to learn.

I was only fifteen then and many more years were to pass before I knew how to stand my ground before him. What I should have told him then was that he had not sent me anywhere. I was in that school only because I was able to win a scholarship. It was the same when I went to the University.

The trouble with my father was his endless desire for wives and children. Or perhaps I should say children and wives. Right now he has five wives—the youngest a mere girl whom he married last year. And he is at least sixty-eight, possibly seventy. He gets a small pension which would be adequate for him if he had a small family instead of his present thirty-five children. Of course he doesn't even make any pretence of providing for his family nowadays. He leaves every wife to her own devices. It is not too bad for the older ones like Mama whose grown-up children help to support them; but the younger ones have to find their children's school fees from farming and petty trading.

All the old man does is buy himself a jar of palm-wine every morning and a bottle of schnapps now and again. Recently he had plunged into the politics of our village and was the local chairman of the P.O.P.

My father and I had our most serious quarrel about eighteen months ago when I told him to his face that he was crazy to be planning to marry his fifth wife. In my anger I said he was storing up trouble for others. This was, of course, a most reprehensible remark to make. The meaning was that I didn't expect him to have much longer to live, which was indelicate and wicked. Had Mama not intervened he probably would have pronounced a curse on me. As it was, he satisfied himself by merely vowing never to touch a penny of mine since he must not store up trouble for *me*. Mama persuaded me to sue for peace by going down on my knees to ask forgiveness and making a peace offering of a bottle of schnapps, two bottles of White Horse and a bottle of Martell.

We were now technically at peace and I was going to tell him about my plans for the post-graduate course. But I knew in advance what he would say. He would tell me that I already had more than enough education, that all the important people in the country today—ministers, businessmen, Members of Parliament, etc., did not have half my education. He would then tell me for the hundredth time to leave "this foolish teaching", and look for a decent job in the government and buy myself a car.

As it turned out I arrived in the capital, Bori, exactly one month after Chief Nanga's unexpected invitation. Although I had written a letter to say when I would be arriving and had followed it up with a telegram, I still had a lingering fear as I announced the address rather importantly and settled back in the taxi that morning. I was thinking that a man of Chief Nanga's easy charm and country-wide popularity must throw out that kind of invitation several times each day without giving it much thought. Wasn't I being unreasonable in trying to hold him down to it? Anyhow I had taken the precaution of writing to an old friend, a newly qualified lawyer struggling to set up in private practice. I would watch Nanga's reaction very closely and if necessary move out smartly again on the following day as though that had always been my intention.

When we got to the Minister's residence my fear increased as his one-eyed stalwart stopped the car at the gate and began to look me over.

"Who you want?" he scowled.

"Chief Nanga."

"He give you appointment?"

"No, but . . ."

"Make you park for outside. I go go haskam if he want see you. Wetin be your name?"

Fortunately the Minister, who was apparently relaxing with his family in the lounge came to the door, and on seeing us rushed outside and threw his arm round me. Then his wife and three of his children trooped out and joined in the excited welcoming.

"Come right inside," said the Minister. "We have been waiting for you all morning. The house is yours."

I hung back to pay the taxi-driver. "No, no, no!" cried my host. "Go right inside. I will settle with the driver. He na my very good friend, no be so, driver?"

"Yes, sir, master," said the driver, who had hitherto seemed a most unfriendly man to me. Now he broke into a broad smile showing smoke- and kola-stained teeth.

For a mother of seven, the eldest of whom was sixteen or seventeen, Mrs Nanga was and still is very well kept. Her face, unlike her husband's had become blurred in my memory. But on seeing her now it all came back again. She was bigger now of course—almost matronly. Her face was one of the friendliest I had ever seen.

She showed me to the Guest's Suite and practically ordered me to have a bath while she got some food ready.

"It won't take long," she said, "the soup is already made."

A small thing, but it struck me even as early as this: Mr Nanga always spoke English or pidgin; his children, whom I discovered went to expensive private schools run by European ladies spoke impeccable English, but Mrs Nanga stuck to our language—with the odd English word thrown in now and again.

My host did not waste time. At about five o'clock that after-noon he told me to get ready and go with him to see the Hon. Simon Koko, Minister for Overseas Training. Earlier that day one of those unseasonal December rains which invariably brought on the cold harmattan had fallen. It had been quite heavy and windy and the streets were now littered with dry leaves, and sometimes half-blocked by broken-off tree branches; and one had to mind fallen telegraph and high-voltage electric wires.

Chief Koko, a fat jovial man wearing an enormous home-knitted red-and-yellow sweater was about to have coffee. He asked if we would join him or have some alcohol.

"I no follow you black white-men for drink tea and coffee in the hot afternoon," said Chief Nanga. "Whisky and soda for me and for Mr Samalu."

Chief Koko explained that nothing warmed the belly like hot coffee and proceeded to take a loud and long sip followed by a satisfied Ahh! Then he practically dropped the cup and saucer on the drinks-table by his chair and jumped up as though a scorpion had stung him.

"They have killed me," he wailed, wringing his hands, breathing hard and loud and rolling his eyes. Chief Nanga and I sprang up in alarm and asked together what had happened. But our host kept crying that *they* had killed him and they could now go and celebrate.

"What is it, S.I.?" asked Chief Nanga, putting an arm around the other's neck.

"They have poisoned my coffee," he said, and broke down completely. Meanwhile the steward, hearing his master's cry, had rushed in.

"Who poisoned my coffee?" he asked.

"Not me-o!"

"Call the cook!" thundered the Minister. "Call him here. I will kill him before I die. Go and bring him."

The steward dashed out again and soon returned to say the cook had gone out. The Minister slumped into his chair and began to groan and hold his stomach. Then his bodyguard whom we had seen dressed like a cowboy hurried in from the front gate, and hearing what had happened dashed out at full speed to try and catch the cook.

"Let's go and call a doctor," I said.

"That's right," said Chief Nanga with relief and, leaving his friend, rushed towards the telephone. I hadn't thought about the telephone.

"What is the use of a doctor?" moaned our poisoned host. "Do they know about African poison? They have killed me. What have I done to them? Did I owe them anything? Oh! Oh! Oh! What have I done?"

Meanwhile Chief Nanga had been trying to phone a doctor and was not apparently getting anywhere. He was now shouting threats of immediate sacking at some invisible enemy.

"This is Chief the Honourable Nanga speaking," he was saying. "I will see that you are dealt with. Idiot. That is the trouble with this country. Don't worry, you will see. Bloody fool. . . ."

At this point the cowboy bodyguard came in dragging the cook by his shirt collar. The Minister sprang at him with an agility which completely belied his size and condition.

"Wait, Master," pleaded the cook.

"Wait your head!" screamed his employer, going for him. "Why you put poison for my coffee?" His huge body was quivering like jelly.

"Me? Put poison for master? Nevertheless!" said the cook, side-stepping to avoid a heavy blow from the Minister. Then with surprising presence of mind he saved himself. (Obviously the cowboy had already told him of his crime.) He made for the cup of coffee quickly, grabbed it and drank every drop. There was immediate silence. We exchanged surprised glances.

"Why I go kill my master?" he asked of a now considerably sobered audience. "Abi my head no correct? And even if to say I de craze why I no go go jump for inside lagoon instead to kill my master?" His words carried conviction. He proceeded to explain the mystery of the coffee. The Minister's usual Nescafé had run out at breakfast and he had not had time to get a new tin. So he had brewed some of his own locally processed coffee which he maintained he had bought from OHMS.

There was an ironic twist to this incident which neither of the ministers seemed to notice. OHMS—Our Home Made Stuff—was the popular name of the gigantic campaign which the Government had mounted all over the country to promote the consumption of locally made products. Newspapers, radio and television urged every patriot to support this great national effort which, they said, held the key to economic emancipation without which our hard-won political freedom was a mirage. Cars equipped with loudspeakers poured out new jingles up and down the land as they sold their products in town and country. In the language of the ordinary people these cars, and not the wares they advertised, became known as OHMS. It was apparently from one of them the cook had bought the coffee that had nearly cost him his life.

The matter having been resolved to everyone's satisfaction I began to feel vicariously embarrassed on behalf of Chief Koko. If anyone had asked my opinion I would have voted strongly in favour of our leaving right away. But no one did. Instead Chief Nanga had begun to tease the other.

"But S.I.," he said, "you too fear death. Small thing you begin holler 'they done kill me, they done kill me!' Like person wey scorpion done lego am for him prick."

I saw his face turning towards me no doubt to get me to join in his laughter. I quickly looked away and began to gaze out of the window.

"Why I no go fear?" asked Chief Koko laughing foolishly. "If na you you no go piss for inside your trouser?"

"Nonsense! Why I go fear? I kill person?"

They carried on in this vein for quite a while. I sipped my whisky quietly, avoiding the eyes of both. But I was saying within myself that in spite of his present bravado Chief Nanga had been terribly scared himself, witness his ill-tempered, loud-mouthed panic at the telephone. And I don't think his fear had been for Chief Koko's safety either. I suspect he felt personally threatened. Our people have a saying that when one slave sees another cast into a shallow grave he should know that when the time comes he will go the same way.

Naturally my scholarship did not get a chance to be mentioned on this occasion. We drove home in silence. Only once did Chief Nanga turn to me and say: "If anybody comes to you and wants to make you minister, run away. True."

That evening I ate my supper with Mrs Nanga and the children, the Minister having gone out to an embassy reception after which he would go to a party meeting somewhere.

"Any woman who marries a minister," said his wife later as we sat watching TV, "has married worse than a night-watchman."

We both laughed. There was no hint of complaint in her voice. She was clearly a homely, loyal wife prepared for the penalty of her husband's greatness. You couldn't subvert her.

"It must be very enjoyable going to all these embassy parties and meeting all the big guns," I said in pretended innocence.

"What can you enjoy there?" she asked with great spirit. "Nine pence talk and three pence food. 'Hallo, hawa you. Nice to see you again.' All na lie lie."

I laughed heartily and then got up pretending to admire the many family photographs on the walls. I asked Mrs Nanga about this one and that as I gravitated slowly to the one on the radiogram which I had noticed as soon as I had stepped into the house earlier in the day. It was the same beautiful girl as in Chief Nanga's entourage in Anata.

"Is this your sister?" I asked.

"Edna. No, she is our wife."

"Your wife? How?"

She laughed. "We are getting a second wife to help me."

The first thing critics tell you about our ministers' official residences is that each has seven bedrooms and seven bathrooms, one for every day of the week. All I can say is that on that first night there was no room in my mind for criticism. I was simply hypnotized by the luxury of the great suite assigned to me. When I lay down in the double bed that seemed to ride on a cushion of air, and switched on that reading lamp and saw all the beautiful furniture anew from the lying down position and looked beyond the door to the gleaming bathroom and the towels as large as a *lappa* I had to confess that if I were at that moment made a minister I would be most anxious to remain one for ever. And maybe I should have thanked God that I wasn't. We ignore man's basic nature if we say, as some critics do, that because a man like Nanga had risen overnight from poverty and insignificance to his present opulence he could be persuaded without much trouble to give it up again and return to his original state.

A man who has just come in from the rain and dried his body and put on dry clothes is more reluctant to go out again than another who has been indoors all the time. The trouble with our new nation—as I saw it then lying on that bed—was that none of us had been indoors long enough to be able to say "To hell with it". We had all been in the rain together until yesterday. Then a handful of us—the smart and the lucky and hardly ever the best—had scrambled for the one shelter our former rulers left, and had taken it over and barricaded themselves in. And from within they sought to persuade the rest through numerous loudspeakers, that the first phase of the struggle had been won and that the next phase—the extension of our house—was even more important and called for new and original tactics; it required that all argument should cease and the whole people speak with one voice and that any more dissent and argument outside the door of the shelter would subvert and bring down the whole house.

Needless to say I did not spend the entire night on these elevated thoughts. Most of the time my mind was on Elsie.

4

I usually don't mind how late I stay up at night but I do mind getting up too early. I was still fast asleep that first morning in the capital when I heard the Minister's voice. I opened my eyes and tried to smile and say good morning.

"Lazy boy," he said indulgently. "Don't worry. I know you must be dog-tired after yesterday's journey. See you later. I am off to the office now." He looked as bright as a new shilling in his immaculate white robes. And he had only come home at two last night, or rather this morning! The crunching of his tires on the loose gravel drive had waked me up in the night and I had looked at my diamond-faced watch which I often forgot to take off even for my bath. I had just bought it and believed the claim that it was everything-proof. Now I know better. But to return to Chief Nanga. There was something incongruous in his going to the office. It sounds silly to say this of a Cabinet Minister but I could not easily associate him in my mind with a desk and files. He was obviously more suited to an out-of-door life meeting and charming people. But anyhow there he was going off to his Ministry punctually at eight.

Much as I already liked and admired Mrs Nanga, I must confess I was inwardly pleased when she told me as I had my breakfast that she and the children were leaving for Anata in three days. Apparently the Minister insisted that his children must be taken home to their village at least once a year.

"Very wise," I said.

"Without it," said Mrs Nanga, "they would become English people. Don't you see they hardly speak our language? Ask them something in it and they reply in English. The little one, Micah, called my mother 'a dirty, bush woman'."

"Terrible," I said, laughing even though the thing wasn't funny.

"Of course I slapped okro seeds out of his mouth," said Mrs Nanga proudly. "My mother not knowing what he had said began to rebuke me."

"Yes, it is good that you take them home sometimes. When do you come back?"

"After Christmas. You know Eddy's father is going to America in January." Eddy is the name of her first son.

The reason why I felt happy at the news of Mrs Nanga's journey was a natural one. No married woman, however accommodating, would view kindly the sort of plans I had in mind, namely to bring Elsie to the house and spend some time with her. Not even a self-contained guest suite such as I was now occupying would make it look well. Even if Mrs Nanga did not object, Elsie most certainly would. My experience of these things is that no woman, however liberal, wants other women to hold a low opinion of her morals. I am not talking about prostitutes because I don't go in for them.

My host was one of those people around whom things were always happening. I must always remain grateful to him for the insight I got into the affairs of our country during my brief stay in his house. From the day a few years before when

I had left Parliament depressed and aggrieved, I had felt, like so many other educated citizens of our country, that things were going seriously wrong without being able to say just how. We complained about our country's lack of dynamism and abdication of the leadership to which it was entitled in the continent, or so we thought. We listened to whispers of scandalous deals in high places—sometimes involving sums of money that I for one didn't believe existed in the country. But there was really no hard kernel of fact to get one's teeth into. But sitting at Chief Nanga's feet I received enlightenment; many things began to crystallize out of the mist—some of the emergent forms were not nearly as ugly as I had suspected but many seemed much worse. However, I was not making these judgements at the time, or not strongly anyhow. I was simply too fascinated by the almost ritual lifting of the clouds, as I had been one day, watching for the first time the unveiling of the white dome of Kilimanjaro at sunset. I stood breathless; I did not immediately say: "Ah! this is the tallest mountain in Africa", or "It isn't really as impressive as I had expected". All that had to wait.

I had neglected to bring any reading matter with me on my visit to Bori, and the Minister's library turned out to be not quite to my taste. There was a decorative set of an American encyclopaedia, there was *She* by Rider Haggard, and also *Ayesha, or the Return of She;* then there were a few books by Marie Corelli and Bertha Clay—I remember in particular *The Sorrows of Satan.* That was all really except for a few odds and ends like *Speeches: How to Make Them.*

I flipped through a few volumes of the encyclopaedia and settled down to read the daily newspapers more closely than I had ever done. And believe me I discovered I had been missing a lot of fun. There was, for instance, this notice inserted into the *Daily Chronicle* by the City Clerk of Bori:

> The attention of the Public is hereby drawn to Section 12 of the Bori (Conservancy) Bye-laws, 1951:
>
> (i) Occupiers of all premises shall provide pails for excrement; the

size of such pails and the materials of which they are constructed shall be approved by the City Engineer.

(ii) The number of such pails to be provided in any premises shall be specified by the City Engineer.

The Public are warned against unauthorized increases in the number of pails already existing on their premises.

The surprises and contrasts in our great country were simply inexhaustible. Here was I in our capital city, reading about pails of excrement from the cosy comfort of a princely seven bathroom mansion with its seven gleaming, silent action, water-closets!

Most of my life (except for a brief interlude at the University where I first saw water-closets) I'd used pit-latrines like the one at what was then my house in Anata. As everyone knows, pit-latrines are not particularly luxurious or ultra-modern but with reasonable care they are adequate and clean. Bucket latrines are a different matter altogether. I saw one for the first time when I lived as a house-boy with an elder half-sister and her husband in the small trading town of Giligili. I was twelve then and it was the most squalid single year of my life. So disgusting did I find the bucket that I sometimes went for days on end without any bowel evacuation. And then there was that week when all the night-soil men in the town decided to go on strike. I practically went without food. As the local inhabitants said at the time, you could "hear" the smell of the town ten miles away.

The only excitement I remember in Giligili was our nightly war on rats. We had two rooms in the large iron-roofed house with its earth walls and floor. My sister, her husband and two small children slept in one and the rest of us—three boys—shared the other with bags of rice, garri, beans and other food-stuff. And, of course, the rats.

They came and sank their holes where the floor and the walls met. As soon as night fell they emerged to eat the grains while we sat around the open fire in the kitchen. You could never get at them because as soon as you entered the room with a lamp they flew into their two holes. We tried getting them with the little iron traps the blacksmiths made, on which you attached a bait—usually a small piece of dried fish. But after one or two of them got killed the rest learned to avoid that fishy bait.

It was then we decided to go hunting. I, or one of the others, would tiptoe in the dark and quietly plug the holes with pieces of rag while the rest waited outside with sticks. After a reasonable interval those outside would charge in with a lamp, slam the door and the massacre would begin. It worked very well. As a rule we did not kill the very small ones; we saved them up for the future. . . . Now all that seemed half a century away.

When Chief Nanga came back to lunch just before two it was clear his mind was preoccupied with something or other. His greeting, though full of warmth as ever, was too brief. He went straight to the telephone and called some ministerial colleague. I soon gathered that it was the Minister of Public Construction.

The conversation made little sense to me at the time especially as I heard only one end of it. But my host spoke with great feeling, almost annoyance, about a certain road which had to be tarred before the next elections. Then I heard the figure of two hundred and ten thousand pounds. But what really struck me was when my Minister said to his colleague:

"Look T.C. we agreed that this road should be tarred. What is this dillying and dallying . . . ? Which expert? So you want to listen to expert now? You know very well T.C. that you cannot trust these our boys. That is why I always say that I prefer to deal with Europeans . . . What? Don't worry about the Press; I will make sure that they don't publish it. . . ."

When he finally put down the phone he said, "Foolish man!" to it and then turned to me.

"That was Hon. T. C. Kobino. Very stupid man. The Cabinet has approved the completion of the road between Giligili and Anata since January but this foolish man has been dillying and dallying, because it is not in his constituency. If it was in his constituency he would not listen to experts. And who is the expert? One small boy from his town—whom we all helped to promote last year. Now the boy advises him that my road should not be tarred before next dry season because he wants to carry out tests in the soil. He has become an earthworm." I laughed at this. "Have you ever heard of such a thing? Is this the first road we are tarring in this country? You see why I say that our people are too selfish and too jealous. . . ."

I got to know a lot about this road which, incidentally, passes through my own village of Urua. At the time I was naturally sympathetic to Chief Nanga's plans for it, if not with his contempt for expert advice. But of course Chief Nanga said the fellow hadn't been appointed in the first place for his expertise at all. And so it went round and round. But none of these things was real news to me, only his saying that he had ordered ten luxury buses to ply the route as soon as it was tarred. Each would cost him six thousand pounds. So he had two good reasons for wanting the road tarred—next elections and the arrival of his buses.

"It doesn't mean I have sixty thousand pounds in the bank," he hastened to add. "I am getting them on never-never arrangement from the British Amalgamated."

I wasn't too sure of the meaning of never-never at that time and I suppose I had a vague idea that the buses were a free gift, which in the circumstances would not have been beyond the British Amalgamated.

After a heavy lunch of pounded yam I was feeling very drowsy. As a rule I always slept in the afternoon but in Chief Nanga's house, where things tumbled over one another in a scramble to happen first, an afternoon snooze seemed most improper, if not shameful. And I thought if Chief Nanga could get home at two in the morning, be at his desk at eight and come back at two looking as fresh as a newly-hatched chick why should I, a child of yesterday by comparison, indulge in such a decadent and colonial habit as taking a siesta? So I bravely dozed in my chair while my host and his wife talked about her journey home. She asked if he had found a cook yet to do his meals while she was away and he said he had asked someone to send one or two along in the evening. Only then did it strike me that they had no cook, only a steward. I wondered how they managed with their dinner parties.

A car drew up outside and a young American couple breezed in. Or rather the wife breezed in and the husband followed in her wake.

"Hi Micah, hi Margaret," said the woman.

"Hi Jean, hi John," replied the Minister whom I had never heard anyone call Micah until then. But he seemed quite pleased, actually. I was greatly shocked. These two people were no older than I and yet had the impudence to call Chief Nanga his now almost forgotten Christian name. But what shocked me even more was his reaction. I had turned quickly and anxiously to watch his face contort with fury. But no. He had replied sweetly, "Hi Jean, hi John." I couldn't understand. I was dead certain that if I or any of our people for that matter had called him Micah he would have gone rampaging mad. But perhaps I shouldn't have been so surprised. We have all accepted things from white skins that none of us would have brooked from our own people.

Mrs Nanga whose Christian name I hadn't even known until now seemed less happy. She said, "Hallo, hallo," and almost immediately withdrew, her frock caught in the parting of her buttocks.

While Jean flirted eagerly with Micah, I was having some very serious discussions with her husband, who it appeared was one of a team of experts at that time advising our government on how to improve its public image in America. He seemed the quiet type and, I thought, a little cowed by his beautiful, bumptious wife. But I had no doubt they were both in their different ways excellent ambassadors. He certainly proved most eloquent when the inevitable subject came up at last—not, I might add, thanks to me.

"We have our problems," he said, "like everyone else. Some of my people are narrow as a pin—we have to admit it.

But at the same time we have gotten somewhere. No one is satisfied, but we have made progress." He gave some facts and figures about lynching which I don't remember now. But I do remember his saying that lynching was not racial in origin and that, up to a certain year like 1875 or something, there had been more whites lynched than Negroes. And I remember too his saying that in five of the last ten years there had been no lynchings at all. I noticed he did not say the last five years.

"So you see, Mr . . . I'm sorry I didn't catch your first name?"

"Odili."

"Odili—a beautiful sound—may I call you by that?"

"Sure," I said, already partly Americanized.

"Mine is John. I don't see why we should call one another Mister this and Mister that—like the British."

"Nor do I," I said.

"What I was saying," he went on, "is that we do not pretend to be perfect. But we have made so much progress lately that I see no cause for anyone to despair. What is important is that we must press on. We must not let up. We just must not be caught sleeping on the switch again . . ."

I was still savouring the unusual but, I thought, excellent technological imagery when I heard as though from faraway John's voice make what I call an astounding claim. I don't mean it was necessarily false—I simply don't know enough history to say.

"America may not be perfect," he was saying, "but don't forget that we are the only powerful country in the entire history of the world, the only one, which had the power to conquer others and didn't do it."

I must have looked more surprised than I felt. The claim did not as yet strike me with its full weight. I was thinking that this unique act of magnanimity must have happened in a small corner of the world long ago.

"Yes," said John, "in 1945 we could have subdued Russia by

placing one atom bomb on Moscow and another on Leningrad. But we didn't. Why? Well, don't ask me. I don't know. Perhaps we are naïve. We still believe in such outdated concepts like freedom, like letting every man run his show. Americans have never wished to be involved in anyone else's show. . . ."

As I have suggested, there is something in Chief Nanga's person which attracts drama irresistibly to him. Memorable events were always flying about his stately figure and dropping at his feet, as those winged termites driven out of the earth by late rain dance furiously around street lamps and then drop panting to the ground.

Here you have John speaking high monologue to me while his wife seems ready, judging by the look in her eyes, to drag Chief Nanga off to bed in broad daylight. Then a knock at the door and a young man in heavily starched white shorts and shirt comes in to offer his services as a cook.

"Wetin you fit cook?" asked Chief Nanga as he perused the young man's sheaf of testimonials, probably not one of them genuine.

"I fit cook every European chop like steak and kidney pie, chicken puri, misk grill, cake omelette. . . ."

"You no sabi cook African chop?"

"Ahh! That one I no sabi am-o," he admitted. "I no go tell master lie."

"Wetin you de chop for your own house?" I asked, being irritated by the idiot.

"Wetin I de chop for my house?" he repeated after me. "Na we country chop I de chop."

"You country chop no be Africa chop?" asked Chief Nanga.

"Na him," admitted the cook. "But no be me de cook am. I get wife for house."

My irritation vanished at once and I joined Chief Nanga's laughter. Greatly encouraged the cook added:

"How man wey get family go begin enter kitchen for make bitterleaf and egusi? Unless if the man no get shame."

We agreed with him but he lost the job because Chief Nanga

preferred bitterleaf and egusi to chicken puri—whatever that was. But I must say the fellow had a point too. As long as a man confined himself to preparing foreign concoctions he could still maintain the comfortable illusion that he wasn't really doing such an unmanly thing as cooking.

5

Jean and John had invited the Minister and me to an informal dinner on the very Saturday Mrs Nanga left for home. Unfortunately John had had to fly to Abaka at short notice to be present at the opening of a new cement factory built with American capital.

In the afternoon Jean phoned to remind us that the party was still on regardless. The Minister promised that we would be there.

But just before seven a most sophisticated-looking young woman had driven in and knocked down all our plans. Chief Nanga introduced her as Barrister Mrs Akilo, and she had come that very minute from another town eighty miles away. She said she hadn't even checked in at the hotel or washed off the dust of the journey. I thought she was beautiful enough with the dust on and I remembered the proverbial joke in my village about a certain woman whose daughter was praised for her beauty and she said: "You haven't seen her yet; wait till she's had a bath."

"Are you in private practice?" I asked Mrs Akilo as Chief Nanga went to answer the phone.

"Yes, my husband and I practise jointly."

"Oh, he is a lawyer too?" I asked.

"Yes, we own a firm of solicitors."

I must confess to a certain feeling of awkwardness before her sophisticated, assured manner. The way she spoke she must have spent her childhood in England. But this awkward feeling was only momentary. After all, I told myself, Chief Nanga who was barely literate was probably going to sleep with her that night.

"Look, Agnes, why don't you use my wife's bedroom instead of wasting money," said Chief Nanga getting back to his seat. "She travelled home today." His phonetics had already moved up two rungs to get closer to hers. It would have been pathetic if you didn't know that he was having fun.

"Thank you, M.A. But I think I had better go to the International. Maybe you could come and pick me up for dinner?"

"Certainly—at what time?"

"Eightish, to give me time to wash and put my feet up for a few minutes."

I was naturally beginning to fear that I was going to be left alone in an empty seven bedroom mansion on a Saturday night. I thought my host had clean forgotten our dinner appointment. But he hadn't. As soon as Mrs Akilo left he said he would take me to the other place before going to the International and he was sure Jean would bring me back. "Agnes is She who must be obeyed," he quoted.

I wondered whether he would also quote Rider Haggard—or whoever wrote those memorable words—to Jean, but all he said was that something urgent had cropped up. Jean was naturally very disappointed. Still she agreed with her characteristic eagerness to run me home at the end of the party, or get some other guest to do so.

The dinner would have come into the category which Mrs Nanga called "nine pence talk and three pence chop". But the talk wasn't bad. Jean started us all off nicely by declaring ecstatically that one of the most attractive things about Chief Nanga apart from his handsomeness was his unpredictability.

"If you ask him if he is coming to dinner he says *I will try.*"

"How sweet!" said a middle-aged woman, I think British, matching her words with a gentle sideways tilt of the head in my direction. "I just love *pidgin* English."

"I will try," Jean continued, "can mean a whole lot of things. It may mean that he won't come—like tonight—or that he might turn up with three other people."

"How intriguing," said the other woman again. And it was only then I began to suspect she was being sarcastic.

Apart from Jean and me there were five others in the room—the British woman and her husband, a middle-aged American Negro writing a book about our country and a white American couple.

Dinner was rice and groundnut stew with chicken. I found it altogether too heavy for that time of day. But the sweet was very good, perhaps on account of its being new to me. I don't remember now what they called it. As for coffee I never touch it at night, unless I have reason for wanting to keep awake. At the University we used to call it the academic nightcap.

The talk, as I said, was very good. My closeness to the Minister gave everything I said heightened significance. And—I don't know whether this happens to other people, but the knowledge that I am listened to attentively works in a sort of virtuous circle to improve the quality of what I say. For instance when at a certain point the conversation turned on art appreciation I made what I still think was a most valid and timely intervention.

One of our leading artists had just made an enormous wooden figure of a god for a public square in Bori. I had not seen it yet but had read a lot about it. In fact it had attracted so much attention that it soon became fashionable to say it was bad or un-African. The Englishman was now saying that it lacked something or other.

"I was pleased the other day," he said, "as I drove past it

to see one very old woman in uncontrollable rage shaking her fists at the sculpture . . ."

"Now that's very interesting," said someone.

"Well, it's more than that," said the other. "You see this old woman, quite an illiterate pagan, who most probably worshipped this very god herself; unlike our friend trained in European art schools; this old lady is in a position to know . . ."

"Quite."

It was then I had my flash of insight.

"Did you say she was shaking her fist?" I asked. "In that case you got her meaning all wrong. Shaking the fist in our society is a sign of great honour and respect; it means that you attribute power to the person or object." Which of course is quite true. And if I may digress a little, I have, since this incident, come up against another critic who committed a crime in my view because he transferred to an alien culture the same meanings and interpretation that his own people attach to certain gestures and facial expression. This critic, a Frenchman writing in a glossy magazine on African art said of a famous religious mask from this country: "Note the half-closed eyes, sharply drawn and tense eyebrow, the ecstatic and passionate mouth . . ."

It was simply scandalous. All that the mask said, all that it felt for mankind was a certain superb, divine detachment and disdain. If I met a woman in the street and she looked at me with the face of that mask that would be its meaning.

But to return to the dinner party. Having demolished the art pundit I felt my reputation soar. I became more than just someone spending his holidays with the Minister of Culture. The white American couple—especially the wife—practically hung on my every word. They wanted to know whether I had trained in Britain, what I had read at the University, what I taught at the Anata Grammar School, had I been to the United States, what did I think of Americans? etc. etc.

But the best story of that evening came from the Negro writer. He told us how a white American had once come up to his lunch table at the International Hotel which, as everyone knows, is a kind of international mart for the sale to our people of all kinds of foreign wares, from ideologies to tractors. This white American came up and said, full of respect:

"May I join you, sir?"

"Sure," replied the other.

"What do you think of the Peace Corps?"

"I've nothing against it. One of my daughters is in it."

"You American?"

"Sure. I came over. . . ."

I thought this was good. I could see the other man promptly excusing himself and searching other tables for *authentic* Africans.

When dinner was over the American Negro offered to drop me off and save Jean the trouble but she wouldn't hear of it, much to my relief I must say. She said she had promised the Minister to deliver me personally safe and sound at his doorstep and in any case she wanted a bit of fresh air before turning in.

And so the others left—almost in a bunch. "I guess we better be going," said Jean, clasping her hands above her head and stretching.

"But we've hardly said a word to each other," I said. Jean went and put on a record, a long-play highlife and we began to dance. I must say she had learned to do the highlife well except that like many another foreign enthusiast of African rhythm she tended to overdo the waist wiggle. I don't say I found it unpleasant—quite on the contrary; I only make a general point, which I think is interesting. It all goes back to what others have come to associate us with. And let it be said that we are not entirely blameless in this. I remember how we were outraged at the University to see a film of breast-throwing, hip-jerking, young women which a neighbouring African state had made and was showing abroad as an African ballet. Jean probably saw it in America. But whatever the case her present effort though pleasing and suitable in the circumstances was by no means good highlife which in essence might carry the same message, but not in this heavy, unsubtle, altogether unsophisticated way.

While we danced I had a quick lesson in psychology. Apparently Jean had noticed while we talked after dinner that I was shaking my legs, which meant that I wanted so badly to go to bed with some woman.

"Was it me or Elsie you wanted?"

"Elsie?"

"Yes, the American couple—Elsie Jackson."

"Oh, I see. No, it wasn't her at all. Good Lord, no. It was you." Which was true.

Actually the leg-shaking business was entirely news to me, the interpretation of it, I mean. As far as I could remember I had always done it and when I was a little boy Mama used to rebuke me for courting epilepsy.

I don't remember whether we danced more than one number on the LP—I very much doubt it. What I remember clearly was the sudden ringing of the bedside telephone. If someone had tiptoed up the stairs in the dark and stuck a knife in my back it couldn't have hit me more.

"Don't move," commanded Jean, bracing me firmly from below with a surprisingly strong pair of arms. I obeyed.

Then with me and all on her she began to wriggle on her back towards the telephone.

She picked up the receiver and called her name. Had she just taken holy communion and been returning to her pew her manner couldn't have appeared more calm and relaxed.

"Hi, Elsie. . . . No, you're welcome. . . . I'm glad you enjoyed it. I got him home all right . . . I was just getting back . . ."

She hung up and put all her suppressed anger in calling Elsie a bitch at which we both convulsed with laughter.

"All she wants to know is if you're still here."

"Do you think she knows?"

"I don't think so and don't care."

Later, much later, we went down hand in hand to the kitchen for Jean to make coffee. I didn't mind drinking it then.

"Sex means much more to a woman than to a man," said Jean reflectively stirring her cup.

"Does it?"

"Sure. It takes place *inside* her. The man uses a mere projection of himself."

"I see."

I wished I could tell her to stop chattering but I didn't know her enough yet. I don't mind people talking before or during it, but I do object most strongly to a post-mortem. One should drink coffee silently or smoke or just sit. Or if one must talk then choose some unrelated subject. I think Jean sensed my feeling; she was such a clever woman.

It was about one-thirty when I caught her trying to suppress a yawn.

"I think I had better be going. Sorry to take you out at this time of night."

"Don't be so British," she said almost vehemently. I wondered what was so British about what I had just said and why it should hurt her so much, but decided against pursuing the matter. As she looked for her car key she asked if I must get back right away or would I like to come with her for a short drive through the town.

"Bori at night is simply fascinating," she said.

"But aren't you tired?"

"You bet I'm not."

She certainly knew the city well, from the fresh-smelling, modern water-front to the stinking, maggoty interior.

"How long have you been in this country?" I asked in undisguised admiration.

"Eleven months," she said. "If you like a place it doesn't take very long to know it."

We drove through wide, well-lit streets bearing the names of our well-known politicians and into obscure lanes named after some unknown small fish. Even insignificant city councillors (Jean apparently knew them all) had their little streets—I remember one called Stephen Awando Street. Going through some of these back streets would have convinced me, had I needed convincing, that the City Clerk's notice about pails was indeed a live issue.

I began to wonder whether Jean actually enjoyed driving

through these places as she claimed she did or whether she had some secret reason, like wanting me to feel ashamed about my country's capital city. I hardly knew her but I could see she was that kind of person, a most complicated woman.

We were now back in the pleasant high-class area.

"That row of ten houses belongs to the Minister of Construction," she said. "They are let to different embassies at three thousand a year each."

So what, I said within myself. Your accusation may be true but you've no right to make it. Leave it to us and don't contaminate our cause by espousing it.

"But that's another Chief Nanga Street," I said aloud, pointing to my left.

"No. What we saw near the fountain was Chief Nanga Avenue," she said and we both burst out laughing, friends again. "I'm not sure there isn't a *Road* as well somewhere," she said. "I know there is a Circle."

Then I promptly recoiled again. Who the hell did she think she was to laugh so self-righteously. Wasn't there more than enough in her own country to keep her laughing all her days? Or crying if she preferred it?

"I have often wondered," she said completely insensitive to my silent resentment, "why don't they call some streets after the many important names in your country's history or past events like your independence as they do in France and other countries?"

"Because this is not France but Africa," I said with peevish defiance. She obviously thought I was being sarcastic and laughed again. But what I had said was another way of telling her to go to hell. Now I guessed I knew why she took so much delight in driving through our slums. She must have taken hundreds of photographs already to send home to her relations. And, come to think of it, would she—lover of Africa that she was—would she be found near a black man in her own country?

"When do you expect John back?" I asked, burning with anger.

"Wednesday. Why?"

"I was wondering whether I could see you again."

"Do you want to?"

"Sure."

"Why not? Let me call you tomorrow?"

6

Anyone who has followed this story at all carefully may well be wondering what had become of the Elsie whom I said was one of my chief reasons for going to Bori. Well, that chief reason had not altered in the least. I had in fact written to her as soon as I had arrived and then paid her a visit at the hospital on the following Saturday morning. But she was still on night-duty and had been waked up from sleep—against the rules of her hospital—to see me. So that first visit had had to be very short. Actually the reason I went at all was to confirm that she was coming to the house to spend the two free days she would earn after the night-shift and that she was bringing a friend of hers along for Chief Nanga, although we did not spell it out so crudely.

In our country a long American car driven by a white-uniformed chauffeur and flying a ministerial flag could pass through the eye of a needle. The hospital gateman had promptly levered up the iron barrier and saluted. The elderly male nurse I beckoned to had sprinted forward with an agility that you would think had left him at least a decade ago. And as I said earlier, although it was against all the laws of the hospital they had let me into the female nurses' quarters and waked up Elsie to see me.

Although she was obviously very drowsy her unconcealed pleasure tempted me very strongly to stay longer than was reasonable or fair. Her sleeping head-tie hooded her face almost down to the eyebrows and completely covered both ears. But despite this and the sleep-swollen eyes she was as desirable as ever. And she was ready—it was just like her—to start rushing around looking for a soft drink and biscuits for me. I refused quite firmly.

In fact I was already on my feet when the other girl came in to greet me. She obviously did not feel as confident as Elsie about her looks and had taken time to touch up. I tried very hard but could not recollect her face at all, even though Elsie said she had introduced us at a university party. She was reasonably good-looking but in that pointed mandibular way that made me think of the talkative weaver bird. Yet she hardly said a word; and when I finally rose to go she did not even go with us to the car outside. Strangely uncurious for one of our women, I thought.

As Elsie and I walked to the car I said humorously:

"I hope Chief Nanga won't ask for a swop."

"For what?" she asked with a puzzled look. Then it occurred to me that she might never have heard that word and so I explained, and we laughed.

"I thought you meant the cotton-wool we use in the theatre," she said, and we laughed again. Then she remembered to add graciously that a swop would not be necessary as her friend was the more beautiful of the two.

"If you are looking for flattery from me this afternoon you won't get it," I said, stooping at the door which the chauffeur had been holding open since I first emerged from the night nurses' dormitory.

"By the way," I said backing out and straightening up

again, "I met an American lady called Elsie at a party the other night. . . . Whenever her name was called—my mind went to you."

"Who tell am say na Elsie be im name? When you see am again make you tell am say im own Elsie na counterfeit. But Odili, you self na waa! How you no even reach Bori finish you done de begin meet another Elsie for party? Make you take am je-je-o."

"Relax," I said, imitating Jean. "What is wrong in telling you I met your namesake at a party?" Actually I was pleased to see Elsie jealous. I meant to go on to say, and had in fact half opened my mouth to begin saying, that she needn't worry, that the other Elsie was no patch on her. But I quickly changed my mind for tactical reasons. Instead I said that if I wanted a second girl-friend I would pick one with a different name if only to avoid confusion.

"Na lie," she said, smiling her seductive, two-dimpled smile. "The way I look you eye I fit say that even ten Elsies no fit belleful you."

"Nonsense," I said. "Abi dem take Elsie make juju for me?" I asked, laughing.

"I know?" she shrugged.

"You suppose to know," I said.

The chauffeur dropped a very broad—and rude—hint at this point by shutting my door again. I chose to ignore him.

"Wetin be the name of your friend's car?"

"Cadillac."

"Ah! This na the famous Cadillac? I no think say I done see am before." She was full of girlish excitement. "Na tough car! Eje-je-je! You think say these people go go another heaven after this?"

"My sister I no know-o. Any way make we follow them chop small for dis world." I opened the door myself and went in, and she helped close it. "I'll be here on Thursday then—at four. Run along now and sleep, darling." I sat back with a proprietary air unusual for me. She stood waving until we disappeared round the bend.

That Thursday evening at six the Minister was due to open the first ever book exhibition of works by local authors. I was specially interested in it because I had ambitions to write a novel about the coming of the first white men to my district.

He came back for lunch at around two-thirty clutching the speech they had prepared for him. Apparently he had been so busy at the office that he hadn't had time to look at it at all. So I thought he was going to sit down now and quickly run through it; but no, he put the file away on top of a book-shelf and began to ask about *our* trip to the hospital. I hadn't realized till then—and perhaps Chief Nanga himself hadn't—that he was going with me.

"I hope they will be ready when we get there. . . ."

"Yes. I told Elsie you had to be at this other place at six."

"Tell me something, Odili. How serious are you about this girl Elsie?"

"You mean about marriage. . . . Good Lord, no! She is just a good-time girl."

"Kabu—Kabu?" he asked with a twinkle in his eye.

"Yes, sort of," I said.

Although what I said about marriage was true enough yet it was grossly unfair at that stage in my relationship with Elsie to call her simply a good-time girl. I suppose what happened was that Chief Nanga and I having already swopped many tales of conquest I felt somehow compelled to speak in derogatory terms about women in general. In fact I had already told the story of my first meeting with Elsie without however identifying her. Naturally Chief Nanga had five stories to every one of mine. The best I thought was about the young married woman who never took her brassière off. It was not until after many encounters that Chief Nanga managed to extract from her that her husband (apparently a very jealous man) had put some juju on her breasts to scare her into faithfulness; his idea being presumably that she would not dare to expose that part of her to another man much less other parts.

"What a fool!" I said. "And he was trying to be so clever."

"E fool pass garri," said Chief Nanga. "Which person tell am na bobby them de take do the thing? Nonsense."

"But that woman na waa," I said. "Who put that kind sense for im head?"

"Woman?" rhapsodized Chief Nanga. "Any person wey tell you say woman no get sense just de talk pure jargon. When woman no want do something e go lef am, but make you no fool yourself say e left the thing because e no get sense for do am."

How true, I thought.

It had been a bit of a surprise to me when Chief Nanga had announced he was coming with me to the hospital. I couldn't very well advise him coldly to stay behind and read through his speech. But I had a strong suspicion he had forgotten all about it and I felt it was only fair that I should remind him. I considered various approaches and then decided on the one that seemed to me to conceal most satisfactorily the small element of self-interest.

"I wish I could help in any way with checking your speech," I said. "But I just cannot read in a moving car."

"Oh! that speech," he said wearily. "I shall finish it in ten minutes; it is not important. If I had known I should have asked my Parliamentary Secretary to go and represent me. Anyhow it's not bad. Talking is now in my blood—from teaching into politics—all na so so talk talk."

Actually I had no serious reason for wanting to go alone. It was true I had formed a pretty clear mental picture of how it was all going to happen, as it were, under my command; but it didn't really matter and certainly wouldn't hurt anyone if it happened differently. For instance, it would have been rather nice sitting between the two girls at the back. Now I would probably sit with the chauffeur. Or better, Elsie and I could sit in front—there was enough space really—and leave the back to the Minister to get acquainted with the other girl.

As it happened all my worry was wasted. The other girl—I don't know what I've done with that girl's name—couldn't come with us on account of a sudden illness. I was very disappointed and a little angry even though Elsie had sworn it was a genuine illness. Fortunately Chief Nanga didn't seem to mind at all, which was hardly surprising for a man who had so many women ready to make themselves available.

I remember him announcing twice or thrice on our way back, with Elsie sitting between us, that he had an important Cabinet meeting which would probably last all night tomorrow, and that he must try and get some sleep tonight. At first I thought he was just showing off to the girl and then I decided it was his wicked way of saying that the coast was completely clear for us. So in my gratitude I began to tell Elsie how little time he spared for himself and his family.

"If somebody wan make you minister," said Chief Nanga, coming to my support, "make you no gree. No be good life."

"Uneasy lies the head that wears the crown," said Elsie.

"Na true, my sister," said the Chief.

"I think I tell you say Chief Nanga de go open book exhibition for six today," I said.

"Book exhibition?" asked Elsie. "How they de make that one again?"

"My sister, make you de ask them for me-o. I be think say na me one never hear that kind thing before. But they say me na Minister of Culture and as such I suppose to be there. I no fit say no. Wetin be Minister? No be public football? So instead for me to sidon rest for house like other people I de go knack grammar for this hot afternoon. You done see this kind trouble before?"

We all laughed, including the driver whose face I could see in the mirror. We joked and laughed all the way back. In Chief Nanga's company it was impossible not to be merry.

We were met outside the exhibition hall by the President of the Writers' Society, a fellow I used to know fairly well at the University. In those days before he became a writer he had seemed reasonably normal to me. But apparently since he published his novel *The Song of the Black Bird*—he had become quite different. I read an interview he gave to a popular magazine in which it came out that he had become so nonconformist that he now designed his own clothes. Judging by his appearance I should say he also tailored them. He had on a white and blue squarish gown, with a round neck and no buttons, over brown, striped, baggy trousers made from the kind of light linen material we sometimes called *Obey the Wind*. He also had a long, untidy beard.

I had expected that in a country where writers were so few they would all be known personally to the Minister of Culture. But it was clear Chief Nanga hadn't even heard the man's name before.

"He is the author of *The Song of the Black Bird*," I said.

"I see," replied Chief Nanga, whose attention was clearly elsewhere at that moment.

"So your society includes musicians as well?" he asked in one fleeting return of interest. But by the time Jalio said "no", his attention had again strayed from us.

"Hello, Jalio," I said, stretching my hand to shake his almost in commiseration. He replied hello and took my hand but obviously he did not remember my name and didn't seem to care particularly. I was very much hurt by this and immediately formed a poor opinion of him and his silly airs.

"You didn't tell me, Mr—er . . ." began the Minister abruptly.

"Jalio, sir."

"Thank you, Mr Jalio. Why didn't you tell me that you are expecting ambassadors at this function?" His eyes were still ranging over the parked cars, some of them carrying diplomatic number plates and two flying flags.

"I am sorry, sir," said Mr Jalio, "but . . ."

"And you come to chairman such an occasion like this?" He accompanied the last two words with an upward movement of a scornful left finger, taking in the whole of Mr Jalio's person. "What part of the country are you?" he asked.

I didn't know what to feel. If Jalio hadn't carried those pretentious airs my sympathies would certainly have stayed with him but now I must confess I was a little pleased to see him deflated.

"Is that what you call national dress in your place?" pursued Chief Nanga mercilessly.

"I dress to please myself, sir," said the writer becoming suddenly defiant.

"Let me tell you," said Chief Nanga in a softened but firm tone. "If you want me to attend any of your functions you must wear a proper dress. Either you wear a suit . . . or if you don't like it you can wear our national costume. That is correct protocol."

It was getting quite embarrassing for me especially when Chief Nanga mentioned a suit and turned to nod approvingly in my direction; for much as I disliked Jalio's pretentiously bizarre habit, still I did not care to be set up as a model of correct dressing.

Then suddenly adopting a paternal and conciliatory tone Chief Nanga reminded us young people that we were the future leaders of our great country.

"I don't care if you respect me or not," he said, "but our people have a saying that if you respect today's king others will respect you when your turn comes. . . . We better go in."

In spite of this inauspicious beginning Mr Jalio went ahead and said many flattering things about Chief Nanga, albeit with a clouded face. He said it was a fitting and appropriate tribute to his concern for African Culture—a concern which was known all over the world—that a university in faraway America was soon to honour him with a doctorate degree.

Chief Nanga stood up magnificently and drew up the sleeves of his robes back to his shoulders with two deft movements of his arms. He did not plunge right away into his prepared script but first made a few remarks of his own. He turned sideways to thank the President of the Writers' Society, looking him over for half a second so that I was afraid he might revert to the subject of dress. Fortunately he did not; he smiled indulgently and a little wickedly and said he was honoured to be invited by Mr Jalio to open the exhibition.

"As you know Mr Jalio is the President of this Society which has already done much to project the African Personality. I believe Mr Jalio himself has composed a brilliant song called . . . erm . . . What is it called again?" he asked Mr Jalio.

Fortunately this was mistaken for witticism and was greeted with loud laughter. It was from her vivacious laugh then that I noticed Jean sitting in the row in front of Elsie and me. Her husband, John, was sitting by her; I hadn't realized he was back. I whispered into Elsie's ear that that was the woman who gave the party I spoke about.

"Is she the famous Elsie?" she whispered back.

"No, her friend."

"So no be only one, even," she said, smiling, "Odi the great." She often shortened my name to Odi.

I didn't listen much to Chief Nanga's speech. When Elsie and I were not whispering into each other's ears I was thinking about the night or even about such irrelevant things as the dress of some of the people in the room. There was one man I noticed particularly. His robes were made from some expensive-looking, European woollen material—which was not so very strange these days. But what surprised me was that the tailor had retained the cloth's thin, yellow border on which the manufacturer advertised in endless and clear black type: 100% WOOL: MADE IN ENGLAND. In fact the tailor had used this advertisement to ornamental advantage on both sleeves. I was struck once again by our people's endless resourcefulness especially when it came to taste in clothes. I noticed that whenever the man hitched up his sleeves which he did every two or three minutes he did it very carefully so that the quality of his material would not be lost in the many rich folds of the dress. He also wore a gold chain round his neck.

7

Chief Nanga was a born politician; he could get away with almost anything he said or did. And as long as men are swayed by their hearts and stomachs and not their heads the Chief Nangas of this world will continue to get away with anything. He had that rare gift of making people feel—even while he was saying harsh things to them—that there was not a drop of ill will in his entire frame. I remember the day he was telling his ministerial colleague over the telephone in my presence that he distrusted our young university people and that he would rather work with a European. I knew I was hearing terrible things but somehow I couldn't bring myself to take the man seriously. He had been so open and kind to me and not in the least distrustful. The greatest criticism a man like him seemed capable of evoking in our country was an indulgent: "Make you no min' am."

This is of course a formidable weapon which is always

guaranteed to save its wielder from the normal consequences of misconduct as well as from the humiliation and embarrassment of ignorance. For how else could you account for the fact that a Minister of Culture announced in public that he had never heard of his country's most famous novel and received applause—as indeed he received again later when he prophesied that before long our great country would produce great writers like Shakespeare, Dickens, Jane Austen, Bernard Shaw and—raising his eyes off the script—Michael West and Dudley Stamp.

At the end of the function Mr Jalio and the Editor of the *Daily Matchet* came forward to congratulate him and to ask for copies of the speech. Chief Nanga produced two clean copies from his file, bent down at the table and amended the relevant portions in his own fair hand by the addition of those two names to the list of famous English writers.

I knew the Editor already from a visit he had paid the Minister a few days earlier. A greasy-looking man, he had at first seemed uneasy about my presence in the room and I had kept a sharp look out for the slightest hint from Chief Nanga to get up and leave them. But no hint was given. On the contrary I felt he positively wanted me to stay. So I stayed. Our visitor took a very long time to come to the point, whatever it was. All I could gather was that he had access to something which he was holding back in Chief Nanga's interest. But it was clear that the Minister did not attach very great importance to whatever it was; in fact he appeared to be sick and tired of the man but dared not say so. Meanwhile the journalist told us one story after another, a disgusting white foam appearing at the corners of his mouth. He drank two bottles of beer, smoked many cigarettes and then got a "dash" of five pounds from the Minister after an account of his trouble with his landlord over arrears of rent. Apparently it was not a straightforward case of debt but, since the landlord and the journalist came from different tribes, the element of tribalism could not be ruled out.

"You see what it means to be a minister," said Chief Nanga as soon as his visitor left. His voice sounded strangely tired and I felt suddenly sorry for him. This was the nearest I had seen him come to despondency. "If I don't give him something now, tomorrow he will go and write rubbish about me. They say it is the freedom of the Press. But to me it is nothing short of the freedom to crucify innocent men and assassinate their character. I don't know why our government is so afraid to deal with them. I don't say they should not criticize—after all no one is perfect except God—but they should criticize constructively. . . ." So that other afternoon when the journalist came forward to get a copy of the speech and shouted: "First rate, sir; I shall put it in the front page instead of a story I have promised the Minister of Construction," I just wondered if he ever suspected where he and his stories would be if Chief Nanga had his way.

It must have been about eight o'clock—it was certainly dark—when we left the exhibition to drive back home. As soon as the car moved I dovetailed my fingers into Elsie's on her lap and threw the other arm across her shoulders in a bold, proprietary gesture.

"That was a beautiful speech and you didn't have much time to go over it," I said, just to get some talk going while privately I throbbed with expectation. An image that had never until then entered my mind appeared to me now. I saw Elsie—or rather didn't see her—as she merged so completely with the darkness of my room, unlike Jean who had remained half undissolved like some apparition as she put her things on in the dark.

"When an old woman hears the dance she knows her old age deserts her," replied Chief Nanga in our language. I laughed more loudly than the proverb deserved and then translated it for Elsie who spoke a different language. We used the laughter to get a little closer so that the arm I had over her shoulder slipped under her arm to her breast, and I pressed her against my side.

When we got back, Chief Nanga and I had whisky while Elsie went upstairs to change.

Incidentally, when on our first return from the hospital Chief Nanga had told his steward to take Elsie's bags to his absent wife's room I had been greatly alarmed. But then I had quickly reassured myself that he was merely displaying great tact and delicacy, and I felt grateful just as I had done when he had told us of the all-night Cabinet meeting.

There was only a short flight of stairs between my room on the ground floor and where Elsie was being installed. When all was silent I would go up quietly, tap on her door, find her waiting and take her downstairs to my room, and we could pretend that our host was none the wiser.

We had an excellent dinner of rice, ripe plantains and fried fish. Elsie, looking ripe and ready in a shimmering yellow dress, took us back to the President of the Writers' Association and his funny garb. I found myself putting up a feeble kind of defence.

"Writers and artists sometimes behave that way," I said.

"I think he will heed my advice," said Chief Nanga. "He is a well-comported young man."

This surprised me a great deal. I suppose it was Jalio's flattering words in introducing the Minister that did it; or more likely Chief Nanga had not missed the almost deferential manner in which one of the ambassadors had approached Jalio with a copy of his book for an autograph. I remember looking at Chief Nanga then and seeing astonishment and unbelief on his face, but I did not think it was enough to persuade him to call Jalio "a well-comported young man" so soon after their clash.

The words "well-comported" struck me almost as forcibly as the sentiment they conveyed. I couldn't say whether it was right or wrong, and in any case you felt once again that such distinctions didn't apply here. Chief Nanga was one of those fortunate ones who had just enough English (and not one single word more) to have his say strongly, without inhibition, and colourfully. I remember his telling me of a "fatal accident" he once had driving from Anata to Bori. Since he was alive I had assumed that someone else had been killed. But as the story unfolded I realized that "fatal" meant no more than "very serious".

I retired soon after dinner so that the others might take

the cue. And Elsie did. The second time I peeped out she was
no longer there in the sitting-room. But Chief Nanga sat on
stolidly looking at the file of the speech he had already given.
Every two minutes or so I came to the door and peeped out
and there he was. Could he be asleep? No, his eyes seemed to
be moving across the page. I was getting quite angry. Why
didn't he take the blessed file to his study? But perhaps what
hurt me most was the fact that I could not muster up sufficient
bravado to step into the sitting-room and up the stairs. Perhaps he even expected me to do so. Let me say that I do not
normally lack resolution in this kind of situation; but Chief
Nanga had, as it were, cramped my style from the very first by
introducing an element of delicacy into the affair, thus making
it not so much a question of my own resolution as of my will-
ingness to parade Elsie before a third person as a common slut.
So there was nothing for it but wait in anger. I sat on my bed,
got up again and paced my room barefoot and in pajamas.

It seemed a full hour before Chief Nanga finally switched
the lights off and turned in. I gave him about five to ten
minutes to settle down in his bed while I had time to steady
myself from the strain of the last hour and the unsettling effect which imminent fulfilment always has on me. Then I began to tiptoe upstairs running my palm up the wooden railing
for guidance. By the time I got to the landing my eyes were
fairly at home in the darkness and it was easy finding Elsie's
door. My hand was already on the knob when I heard voices
within. I was transfixed to the spot. Then I heard laughter and
immediately turned round and went down the stairs again. I
did not go into my room straight away but stood for long minutes in the sitting-room. What went on in my mind at that
time lacked form and I cannot now set it down. But I remember finally deciding that I was jumping to conclusions, that
Chief Nanga had in all probability simply opened the connect-
ing door between the two rooms to say good-night and ex-
change a few pleasantries. I decided to give him a minute or
two more, and then discarding this pussy-footed business go up
boldly and knock on Elsie's door. I went back to my room to

wait, switched on the bedside lamp which was worked by a short silvery rope instead of a normal switch, looked at my watch which I had taken off and put on a bedside stool. It was already past half-past ten. This stung me into activity again. I hadn't thought it was so late. I rushed into the sitting-room and made to bound up the stairs when I heard as from a great distance Elsie deliriously screaming my name.

I find it difficult in retrospect to understand my inaction at that moment. A sort of paralysis had spread over my limbs, while an intense pressure was building up inside my chest. But before it reached raging point I felt it siphoned off, leaving me empty inside and out. I trudged up the stairs in the incredible delusion that Elsie was calling on me to come and save her from her ravisher. But when I got to the door a strong revulsion and hatred swept over me and I turned sharply away and went down the stairs for the last time.

I sat on my bed and tried to think, with my head in my hands. But a huge sledgehammer was beating down on my brain as on an anvil and my thoughts were scattering sparks. I soon realized that what was needed was action; quick, sharp action. I rose to my feet and willed myself about gathering my things into the suitcase. I had no clear idea what I would do next, but for the moment that did not trouble me; the present loomed so large. I brought down my clothes one at a time from the wardrobe, folded them and packed them neatly; then I brought my things from the bathroom and put them away. These simple operations must have taken me a long time to complete. In all that time I did not think anything particularly. I just bit my lower lip until it was sore. Occasionally words like "Good Heavens" escaped me and came out aloud. When I had finished packing I slumped down in the chair and then got up again and went out into the sitting-room to see if the sounds were still coming. But all was now dark and quiet upstairs. "My word!" I remember saying; then I went to wait for Elsie. For I knew she would come down shedding tears of shame and I would kick her out and bang the door after her for ever. I waited and waited and then, strange as it may sound, dozed off. When I started awake I had that dull, heavy terror of knowing that something terrible had happened without immediately remembering what it was. Of course the uncertainty lasted only one second, or less. Recollection and panic followed soon enough and then the humiliating wound came alive again and began to burn more fresh than when first inflicted. My watch said a few minutes past four. And Elsie had not come. My eyes misted, a thing that had not happened to me in God knows how long. Anyway the tears hung back. I took off my pajamas, got into other clothes and left the room by the private door.

I walked for hours, keeping to the well-lit streets. The dew settled on my head and helped to numb my feeling. Soon my nose began to run and as I hadn't brought a handkerchief I blew it into the roadside drain by closing each nostril in turn with my first finger. As dawn came my head began to clear a little and I saw Bori stirring. I met a night-soil man carrying his bucket of ordure on top of a battered felt hat drawn down to hood his upper face while his nose and mouth were masked with a piece of black cloth like a gangster. I saw beggars sleeping under the eaves of luxurious department stores and a lunatic sitting wide awake by the basket of garbage he called his possession. The first red buses running empty passed me and I watched the street lights go off finally around six. I drank in all these details with the early morning air. It was strange perhaps that a man who had so much on his mind should find time to pay attention to these small, inconsequential things; it was like the man in the proverb who was carrying the carcass of an elephant on his head and searching with his toes for a grasshopper. But that was how it happened. It seems that no thought—no matter how great—had the power to exclude all others.

As I walked back to the house I tried in vain to find the kind of words I needed to speak to Chief Nanga. As for Elsie I should have known that she was a common harlot and the less said about her the better.

Chief Nanga was outside his gate apparently looking out for me when I came round the last bend. He happened just then to be looking in the opposite direction and did not see me at once. My first reaction on seeing him was to turn back. Fortunately I did not give in to that kind of panic; in any case he turned round just then, saw me and began to come towards me.

"Where have you been, Odili?" he asked. "We—I—have been looking for you; I nearly phoned nine-nine-nine."

"Please don't talk to me again," I said.

"What . . . ! Wonders will never end! What is wrong, Odili?"

"I said don't talk to me again," I replied as coolly as possible.

"Wonders will never end! Is it about the girl? But you told me you are not serious with her; I asked you because I don't like any misunderstanding. . . . And I thought you were tired and had gone to sleep . . ."

"Look here, Mr Nanga, respect yourself. Don't provoke me any more unless you want our names to come out in the newspapers today." Even to myself I sounded strange. Chief Nanga was really taken aback, especially when I called him mister.

"You have won today," I continued, "but watch it, I will have the last laugh. I never forget."

Elsie was standing at the door with arms folded across her bust when I came in at the gate. She immediately rushed indoors and disappeared.

When I brought out my suitcase Chief Nanga, who had not said another word since I insulted him, came forward and tried to put a hand on my shoulder in one last effort at reconciliation.

"Don't touch me!" I eased my shoulders away like one avoiding a leper's touch. He immediately recoiled; his smile hardened on his face and I was happy.

"Don't be childish, Odili," he said paternally. "After all she is not your wife. What is all this nonsense? She told me there is nothing between you and she, and you told me the same thing . . . But anyway I am sorry if you are offended; the mistake is mine. I tender unreserved apology. If you like I can bring you six girls this evening. You go do the thing sotay you go beg say you no want again. Ha, ha, ha, ha!"

"What a country!" I said. "You call yourself Minister of Culture. God help us." And I spat; not a full spit but a token, albeit unmistakable, one.

"Look here, Odili," he turned on me then like an incensed leopard, "I will not stomach any nonsense from any small boy for the sake of a common woman, you hear? If you insult me again I will show you pepper. You young people of today are very ungrateful. Imagine! Anyway don't insult me again-o. . . ."

"You can't do a damn-all," I said. "You are just a bush . . ." I cut myself short and walked out, lumbering my suitcase past Dogo the one-eyed stalwart who had presumably heard our voices and come out from the Boys' Quarters in his sleeping loin-cloth to investigate.

"Na this boy de halla so for master im face?" I heard him ask.

"Don't mind the stupid idiot," said Chief Nanga.

"E no fit insult master like that here and comot free. Hey! My frien'!" he shouted, coming after me. "Are you there?" His voice was full of menace.

I was then half-way to the outside gate. I turned boldly round but on second thoughts said nothing, turned again and continued.

"Leave am, Dogo. Make e carry im bad luck de go. Na my own mistake for bring am here. Ungrateful ingrate!"

I was now at the gate but his voice was loud and I heard every word.

I took a taxi to my friend Maxwell's address. Maxwell Kulamo, a lawyer, had been my classmate at the Grammar School. We called him Kulmax or Cool Max in those days; and his best friends still did. He was the Poet Laureate of our school and I still remember the famous closing couplet of the poem he wrote when our school beat our rivals in the Intercollegiate Soccer Competition:

Hurrah! to our unconquerable full backs.
(The writer of these lines is Cool Max.)

He was already fully dressed for Court (striped trousers and black coat) and was eating breakfast when I arrived. The few words I spoke to Nanga and the fairly long taxi ride had combined to make it possible for me to wear a passable face.

"Good gracious!" Max shouted, shaking my hand violently. "Diligent! Na your eye be this?" Diligent was a version of Odili I had borne at school.

"Cool Max!" I greeted him in return. "The writer of these lines!" We laughed and laughed and the tears I had not shed last night came to my eyes. Max suspected nothing and even thought I was just coming from home. I told him rather shamefacedly that I had been in town for the past few days but hadn't found it possible to contact him. He took this to be a reference to his having no telephone in the house, a fact which in turn could be a reflection on his practice.

"I have been on the waiting list for a telephone for two months," he said defensively. "You see, I have not given anyone a bribe, and I don't know any big gun . . . So you have been staying with that corrupt, empty-headed, illiterate capitalist. Sorry-o."

"Na matter of can't help," I said. "He na my old teacher, you know."

I was dipping my bread in the cup of hot cocoa drink Max's boy had made for me. Chief Nanga and Elsie already seemed so distant that I could have talked about them like casual acquaintances. But I was not going to delay Max by talking now. And in any case I had no wish to make him think that I only remembered him when I could no longer enjoy the flesh-pots of Chief Nanga's home.

Within minutes I was already feeling so relaxed and at ease here that I wondered what piece of ill-fate took me to Chief Nanga in the first place.

8

It was only after Max had left for Court at around nine that I finally felt the full weight of the previous night's humiliation settling down on me. The heat and anger had now largely evaporated leaving the cold fact that another man had wrenched my girl-friend from my hand and led her to bed under my very eyes, and I had done nothing about it—could do nothing. And why? Because the man was a minister bloated by the flatulence of ill-gotten wealth, living in a big mansion built with public money, riding in a Cadillac and watched over by a one-eyed, hired thug. And as though that were not enough he had had the obscene effrontery to say he thought I was too tired! A man of fifty or more with a son in a secondary school and a wife whose dress gets caught between the buttocks thought I was too tired! And here was I doing nothing about it except speculating whether Elsie would go back to her hospital that day or spend another night with

Chief Nanga. By late afternoon I even had the crazy, preposterous idea of wanting to go to a public telephone to put through an anonymous call. Of course I killed the disgraceful thought right away.

But I suppose it was possible (judging by the way things finally worked themselves out) that these weak and trivial thoughts might have been a sort of smoke screen behind which, unknown to me, weighty decisions were taking shape. It was perhaps like the theory of writing examinations that one of my lecturers used to propound to us. He said the right technique was to read all the questions once through, select those you wanted to answer and then start with the easiest; his theory being that while you were answering the easy number your subconscious would set to work arranging the others for you. I tried it out for my degree examination and although the result was not exactly startling I suppose it could have been worse.

But on the present question of Chief Nanga my subconscious (or something very much like it) seemed to have gone voluntarily into operation. I was just flapping about like a trapped bird when suddenly I saw the opening. I saw that Elsie did not matter in the least. What mattered was that a man had treated me as no man had a right to treat another—not even if he was master and the other slave; and my manhood required that I make him pay for his insult in full measure. In flesh and blood terms I realized that I must go back, seek out Nanga's intended parlour-wife and give her the works, good and proper. All this flashed through my mind in one brief moment of blinding insight—just like that, without warning!

I was singing happily when Max came home in the late afternoon. He tried to be furious with his house-boy for not giving me my share of the lunch when it was ready, but I went straight to the boy's defence and said he had offered to serve me but that I insisted on waiting, which was quite untrue.

As we ate I told Max about Elsie and Chief Nanga, amending the story in several minor particulars and generally making light of it all, not only because I was anxious to play down my humiliation but even more because I no longer cared for anything except the revenge.

"If you put juju on a woman it will catch that old rotter," said Max after I had told the story.

"I know someone who did," I said light-heartedly, "but the old rotter wasn't caught." I then told him the story of the woman who didn't take off her bra, thinking it would amuse him. I was wrong.

"That's all they care for," he said with a solemn face. "Women, cars, landed property. But what else can you expect when intelligent people leave politics to illiterates like Chief Nanga?"

The appearance of comparative peace which Max's house presented to me that morning proved quite deceptive. Or perhaps some of Chief Nanga's "queen bee" characteristics had rubbed off on me and transformed me into an independent little nucleus of activity which I trailed with me into this new place. That first night I not only heard of a new political party about to be born but got myself enrolled as a foundation member. Max and some of his friends having watched with deepening disillusion the use to which our hard-won freedom was being put by corrupt, mediocre politicians had decided to come together and launch the Common People's Convention.

There were eight young people in his room that evening. All but one were citizens of our country, mostly professional types. The only lady there was a very beautiful lawyer who, I learned afterwards, was engaged to Max whom she had first met at the London School of Economics. There was a trade-unionist, a doctor, another lawyer, a teacher and a newspaper columnist.

Max introduced me without any previous consultation as a "trustworthy comrade who had only the other day had his girl-friend snatched from him by a minister who shall remain nameless".

Naturally I did not care for that kind of image or reputation. So I promptly intervened to point out that the woman in question was not strictly speaking my girl-friend but a casual acquaintance whom both Chief Nanga and I knew.

"So it was Chief Nanga, yes?" said the European and every-one burst out laughing.

"Who else could it be?" said one of the others.

The white man was apparently from one of the Eastern Bloc countries. He did not neglect to stress to me in an aside that he was there only as a friend of Max's. He told me a lot of things quietly while the others were discussing some obscure details about the launching. I was as much interested in what he said as the way he said it. His English had an exotic quality occasionally—as when he said that it was good to see intellec-tuals like Max, myself and the rest coming out of their "tower of elephant tusk" into active politics. And he often punctuated whatever he was saying with "yes", spoken with the accent of a question.

I must say that I was immediately taken with the idea of the Common People's Convention. Apart from everything else it would add a second string to my bow when I came to deal with Nanga. But right now I was anxious not to appear to Max and his friends as the easily impressed type. I suppose I wanted to erase whatever impression was left of Max's unfortunate if un-intentional presentation of me as a kind of pitiable jellyfish. So I made what I intended to be a little spirited sceptical speech.

"It is very kind of you gentlemen and lady—I say gentle-men and lady advisedly because this happens to be Africa—it is very kind of you to accept me so readily. I wish to assure you all that your confidence will be fully justified. But without trying to put a cat among your pigeons I must say that I find it somewhat odd that a party calling itself the Common Peo-ple's Convention should be made up of only professional men and women. . . ."

I was interrupted by many voices at once. But the rest gave way to Max.

"That is not entirely accurate, Odili. What you see here is only the vanguard, the planning stage. Once we are ready we shall draw in the worker, the farmer, the blacksmith, the car-penter . . ."

"And the unemployed, of course," said the young lady

with that confidence of a beautiful woman who has brains as well, which I find a little intimidating. "And I'd like to take our friend up on a purely historical point. The great revolutions of history were started by intellectuals, not the common people. Karl Marx was not a common man; he wasn't even a Russian."

The trade-unionist applauded the speech by clapping and shouting "Hear, hear." The rest made different kinds of appreciative noises.

"Well, well," I thought and gave up altogether my next idea of asking how the thing was going to be financed.

"At the same time," said Max, acting the perfect chairman, "I can't say that I blame Odili for making that point. He's always been a stickler for thoroughness. Do you know the name we called him at school? Diligent." Everyone laughed.

"I should add that *he* was called Cool Max," I said. "He always played it cool."

"And still does," said the lady with a wink at him.

"I beg your pardon," protested Max playfully. "Anyhow, lady and gentlemen, or rather, gentlemen and lady, to borrow our friend's fine example . . ."

"Max!" protested the girl in mock outrage. "Well, I never!"

"I think to save all difficulty—yes? we should simply say comrades—yes?" suggested the European, laughing nervously which made me think he wasn't joking like the rest of us.

"Hear! hear!" said the trade-unionist.

"Yes," said Max coolly, "except that as I said several times before, I don't want anybody to say we are communists. We can't afford the label. It would simply finish us. Our opponents would point at us and say, 'Look at those crazy people who want to have everything in common including their wives', and that would be the end of it. That's the plain fact."

"I don't know about that," said the trade-unionist. "I think our trouble in this country is that we are too nervous. We say we are neutral but as soon as we hear communist we begin de shake and piss for trouser. Excuse me," he said to the lady and dropped the pidgin as suddenly as he had slid into it. "The other day somebody asked me why did I go to Russia last January. I told him it was because if you look only in one direction your neck will become stiff. . . ."

We all laughed loud, especially the European.

"I know, Joe . . ." began Max, but Joe did not yield easily.

"No, excuse me, Max," he said, "I am serious. We are either independent in this country or we are not."

"We are not," said Max, and everyone laughed again, including Joe this time, all the heat apparently siphoned off him.

I was struck by Max's cool, sure touch. He was clearly in control of the situation. And he seemed to me to have just the right mixture of faith and down-to-earth practical common sense.

"We will not win the next election," he told me on another occasion. In itself it was a fairly obvious statement; but how many mushroom political parties had we seen spring up, prophesy a landslide victory for themselves and then shrivel up again. "What we must do is get something going," said Max, "however small, and wait for the blow-up. It's bound to come. I don't know how or when but it's got to come. You simply cannot have this stagnation and corruption going on indefinitely."

"How do you propose getting the money?"

"We will get some," he smiled, "enough to finance ordinary election expenses. We will leave mass bribing of the electors to P.O.P. and P.A.P. We will simply drop cats among their pigeons here and there, stand aside and watch. I am right now assembling all the documentary evidence I can find of corruption in high places. Brother, it will make you weep."

"I am sure."

Because I had asked him jokingly as we were about to retire to bed if he still wrote poetry, Max had gone and fished out lines he wrote seven years ago to the music of a famous highlife. He wrote it during the intoxicating months of high hope soon after Independence. Now he sang it like a dirge. And, believe me, tears welled up at the back of my eyes; tears for the dead, infant hope. You may call me sentimental if you like.

I have the poem, "Dance-offering to the Earth-Mother", right here before me as I write and could quote the whole of it; but it could never convey in print the tragic feeling I had that evening as Max sang it tapping his foot to the highlife rhythm, and bringing back vividly the gaiety and high promise of seven years ago which now seemed more than seven lifetimes away!

> I will return home to her—many centuries have I wandered—
> And I will make my offering at the feet of my lovely Mother:
> I will rebuild her house, the holy places they raped and plundered,
> And I will make it fine with black wood, bronzes and terra-cotta.

I read this last verse over and over again. Poor black mother! Waiting so long for her infant son to come of age and comfort her and repay her for the years of shame and neglect. And the son she has pinned so much hope on turning out to be a Chief Nanga.

"Poor black mother!" I said out aloud.

"Yes, poor black mother," said Max looking out of the window. After a long interval he turned round and asked if I remembered my Bible.

"Not really. Why?"

"Well, I can't get it out of my system. You know my father is an Anglican priest. . . . No, when you talked about poor black mother just now I remembered a passage that goes something like this:

> "A voice was heard in Ramah
> Weeping and great lamentation
> Rachel weeping for her children
> And she would not be comforted, because they are not.

"It is a favourite of my father's who, by the way, still thinks we should never have asked the white man to go."

"Perhaps he is right," I said.

"Well, no. The trouble is that he hasn't got very much out of Independence, personally. There simply weren't any white posts in his profession that he could take over. There is only one bishop in the entire diocese and he is already an African."

"You are unfair to the old man," I said laughing.

"You should hear some of the things the old man says about me. I remember when I last went to see him with Eunice he said who knows I might get a son before him. Oh, we crack such expensive jokes."

"You are an only son, aren't you?"

"Yes."

I felt so envious.

"You know, Odili," he began suddenly after a longish pause, "I don't believe in Providence and all that kind of stuff but your arrival just at this very moment is most fortunate. You see, we were planning to appoint able and dynamic organizing secretaries in each of the regions very soon. Now we've got you we don't have to worry our head about the south-east any more."

"I'll do what I can, Max," I said.

Perhaps the most astonishing thing Max told me about the new party was that one of the junior ministers in the Government was behind it.

"What is he doing in the Government if he is so dissatisfied with it?" I asked naïvely. "Why doesn't he resign?"

"Resign?" laughed Max. "Where do you think you are— Britain or something? Don't be funny, Odili."

"I am not being funny," I said hotly, perhaps more hotly than was called for.

I knew very well and needed no reminder that we were not in Britain or something, that when a man resigned in our country it was invariably with an eye on the main chance—as when a few years ago ten newly elected P.A.P. Members of Parliament had switched parties at the opening of the session and given the P.O.P. a comfortable majority overnight in return for ministerial appointments and—if one believed the rumours—a little cash prize each as well. All that was well known, but I would have thought it was better to start our new party clean, with a different kind of philosophy.

"I know how you feel," said Max rather patronizingly. "I felt like that at first. But we must face certain facts. You take a man like Nanga now on a salary of four thousand plus all the—you know. You know what his salary was as an elementary school teacher? Perhaps not more than eight pounds a month. Now do you expect a man like that to resign on a little matter of principle . . . ?"

"Assuming, that is, that he can recognize principle when he sees it," I added somewhat pompously.

"Well, exactly. I am not saying, mark you, that our man is like Nanga. *He* is a true nationalist and would not hesitate to resign if he felt it was really necessary. But as he himself points out, do we commit suicide every day we feel unhappy with the state of the world?"

"It's hardly the same thing," I said.

"Well, I know. But having a man like him right in the Government is very essential, I can assure you. He tells me all that goes on."

"In that sense I suppose you are right. As the saying goes it is only when you are close to a man that you can begin to smell his breath."

"Well, exactly."

9

I returned to Anata on 23rd December after Max and his fiancée, Eunice, had tried in vain to make me spend Christmas in
Bori. The lorry dropped me at the small roadside market
called Waya which had sprung up to serve the Grammar
School. Something unusual seemed to be going on in Josiah's
shop-and-bar. Whatever it was had drawn crowds from the
rest of the market to it. You couldn't say definitely at first
whether it was a good thing or a bad from the loud, excited
talking, but it was soon clear from the kind of gesticulation I
saw that something had gone wrong. I saw one old woman
swing her hand in a gyre round her head and jerk it towards
Josiah's shop, a most ominous sign.

"Teacher," said one villager who had spotted me and was
coming to shake hands. I didn't know him by name. "Are you
back already? Let me carry your box. I hope your home people
are well."

We shook hands and I told him that my home people were well when I left them. Then I asked him what was going on there at the shop.

"What else could it be but Josiah," he said, taking up my box and placing it on his head. "I have said that what the white man's money will bring about has not shown itself yet. You know Azoge?"

"The blind beggar?"

"Yes, the blind beggar. Josiah is not touched by Azoge's ill-fortune and he is not satisfied with all the thieving he does here in the name of trade but must now make juju with Azoge's stick." At this point he turned aside to greet another villager and they both shook their heads over the abomination.

"I don't understand," I said when we resumed our conversation.

"Josiah called Azoge to his shop and gave him rice to eat and plenty of palm-wine. Azoge thought he had met a kind man and began to eat and drink. While he was eating and drinking Josiah took away his stick—have you ever heard such abomination?—and put a new stick like the old one in its place thinking that Azoge would not notice. But if a blind man does not know his own stick, tell me what else would he know? So when Azoge prepared to go he reached for his stick and found that a strange one was in its place, and so he began to shout. . . ."

"I still don't understand. What does Josiah want to do with his stick?"

"How are you asking such a question, teacher? To make medicine for trade, of course."

"That is terrible," I said, still very much in the dark but not caring to make it known.

"What money will do in this land wears a hat; I have said it."

When we got to my house I gave him one shilling and he thanked me, gave a few more unhelpful details of the incident and went to rejoin the crowd. I would have gone there too but was tired from my long journey and in any case my mind was on other things. I meant to rest a little, have a wash and go in search of Mrs Nanga. But the noise outside was getting louder and louder and in the end I had to go out to see.

Josiah had apparently barricaded himself inside his shop, from where, no doubt, he could hear the crowds outside pronouncing deadly curses on him and his trade. The blind man, Azoge, was there still, telling his story over and over again. I walked from one little group to another, listening.

"So the beast is not satisfied with all the money he takes from us and must now make a medicine to turn us into blind buyers of his wares," said one old woman. "May he blind his mother and his father, not me." She circled her head with her right hand and cast the evil towards the shop.

"Some people's belly is like the earth. It is never so full that it will not take another corpse. God forbid," said a palm-wine tapper I knew. I believe he was one of those who supplied Josiah with the wine he retailed in beer-bottles.

But the most ominous thing I heard was from Timothy, a middle-aged man, who was a kind of Christian and a carpenter.

"Josiah has taken away enough for the owner to notice," he said again and again. "If anyone ever sees my feet in this shop again let him cut them off. Josiah has now removed enough for the owner to see him."

I thought much afterwards about that proverb, about the man taking things away until the owner at last notices. In the mouth of our people there was no greater condemnation. It was not just a simple question of a man's cup being full. A man's cup might be full and none be the wiser. But here the owner knew, and the owner, I discovered, is the will of the whole people.

Within one week Josiah was ruined; no man, woman or child went near his shop. Even strangers and mammy-wagon passengers making but a brief stop at the market were promptly warned off. Before the month was out, the shop-and-bar closed for good and Josiah disappeared—for a while.

But to return to the day I came back from Bori: I hired a bicycle in the evening from the repairer in the market and went to see Mrs Nanga. I had to see her before the story of my quarrel with her husband got to Anata and ruined my chances of reaching Edna, the intended "parlour-wife". Not that I thought Chief Nanga himself would want to transmit it although there was no knowing what he might or might not do, but there were many others in Bori who might send it on for want of better news.

She was surprised to see me but I had a convincing explanation ready; sudden change of plans and that kind of thing. Her children came and shook hands. The village, I noticed, had already rubbed off a good deal of their Bori trimness and made their Corona-School English a little incongruous.

"Go and get a drink for Odili," said Mrs Nanga to her eldest son, Eddy—the one at secondary school. He soon brought me a bottle of ice-cold beer which was just the thing after my strenuous ride. I poured the first glass down my throat in one go and then began to sip the second. As I did so I kept wondering how to broach the question of Edna without appearing too suspicious.

"When are you preparing to return to Bori?" I asked. "The house is quite cold without you and the children."

"Don't tell me about Bori, my brother. I want to rest a bit here . . . Eddy's father says I should come back at the end of next month before he goes to America but I don't know. . . ."

"I thought you were going with him?"

"Me?" She laughed.

"Yes. Why not?"

"My brother, when those standing have not got their share you are talking about those kneeling. Have you ever heard of a woman going to America when she doesn't know ABC?"

Fine, I thought, and was about to plunge in, but Mrs Nanga obliged me even more!

"When Edna comes she will go to those places," she said. "I am too old and too bush."

"Who is Edna?"

"Don't you know about Edna, our new wife?"

"Oh, that girl. Nonsense. She doesn't know half as much book as you."

"Ah, she does-o. I no go Modern School."

"But standard six in your time was superior to Senior Cambridge today," I said in our language, refusing to be drawn into the levity of pidgin.

"You talk as though I went to school in nineteen-kridim," she said, somewhat hurt.

"No, no, no," I said. "But education has been falling every year. Last year's standard six is higher than this year's."

But she didn't seem to be all that hurt after all. Her mind appeared to be far away on other thoughts.

"I passed the entrance to a secondary school," she said wistfully, "but Eddy's father and his people kept at me to marry him, marry him, and then my own parents joined in; they said what did a girl want with so much education? So I foolishly agreed. I wasn't old enough to refuse. Edna is falling into the same trap. Imagine a girl straight from college not being allowed to teach even for one year and look around. Anyway what is my share in it? Let her come quick-quick to enjoy Chief Nanga's money before it runs away." She laughed bitterly.

My first reaction was to feel uncomfortable, not so much for what Mrs Nanga had said as by the presence while she said it of her fifteen-year-old son, Eddy.

"Is she coming into the house soon?"

"I don't know. What is my own there? She can come tomorrow as far as I am concerned; the house is there. And she can take over from me and stay awake at night to talk grammar; and in the morning her dress will be smelling of cigarette smoke and white people." I couldn't help laughing.

"Why don't you want to advise her? She should take at least one year and teach and look around. She will listen to you, I'm sure; she is only a little girl, really."

"True? She was born yesterday, eh? Let her come and suck." She indicated her left breast. "No, my brother, I won't spoil anybody's good fortune. When Eddy's father married me I was not half her age. As soon as her mother recovers let her come and eat Nanga's wealth . . . The food is cooked and the smell of the soup is around. Let nobody remember the woman who toiled and starved when there was no money . . ." She rubbed her eyes with a corner of her lappa and blew her nose into it.

"Where is her home? I must go and talk to her—tomorrow morning, I must." Before I said this I considered Eddy's presence but quickly took the calculated risk that he was likely to be on his mother's side, although you couldn't see anything of it on his handsome face, even with his mother on the brink of tears.

"Go if you like," said Mrs Nanga with feigned indifference, "but don't tell anyone I sent you. If I am not to grow bigger let me at least remain as small as I am."

I was right about Eddy. He immediately and carefully described how to get to Edna's home—in another and fairly distant part of the village. He even suggested that the driver take me in their Vauxhall, which showed that in spite of his height he was still a mere boy.

I lost my way a few times before I found Odo's house of red earth and thatched roof. He was sitting in his front room making the rope used for tying yams on to erect poles in the barn. The short pieces of fibre from which he worked lay beside him in three bundles, one of which had become loose at the girdle from depletion. The rope he had made so far was rolled up in a ball lying between his feet; he held its free end in his hand and tied new lengths of fibre to it. When I came in he was strengthening the last knot by pulling hard at it across his chest, exposing his locked teeth in the action. He was a big man with an enormous, shining stomach sitting on the rolled-up portion of his loin-cloth. His eyes were bloodshot and his hair greying.

We shook hands and I took a chair facing him and backing the approaches to the house. He said "welcome" several times more while he worked.

"I must carry the debt of a kolanut," he said, re-tying a

knot that had just come undone under his pull. "It got finished only this morning."

"Don't worry about kolanut," I said, and added after a long
pause: "You do not know me, I'm sure. I am one of the teachers
at the Grammar School."

"Yes," he said looking up. "I knew it was a face I had seen."

We shook hands again and he said "welcome" and apolo-
gized once more for not having kolanuts and I replied that it
was not every day that people had kolanuts.

"Since the woman of the house went into hospital there
hasn't been anyone to look after these things," he said.

"I hope she will become well again soon."

"We are looking on the Man Above."

After a suitable pause I asked about Edna.

"She is cooking the food to take to the hospital," he replied
coldly.

"I have a message for her from my friend Chief Nanga."

"You are a friend of my in-law? Why did you not tell me
so? Have you come from Bori, then?"

"Yes. I came back only yesterday."

"True? How was he when you left him?"

"He was well."

He turned round on his seat, towards a door leading
into inner rooms and raising his voice called out. Edna's voice
came back from the interior of the compound, like a distant
flute.

"Come and salute our guest," hollered her father in the
same loud voice. While we waited, I felt his eyes on me and so
I made a special effort to look as casual as I could. I even
turned round on my seat and inspected the approaches to the
house and then formed my lips as though I was whistling to
myself.

"Has your wife been in the hospital a long time?" I asked.

"Since three weeks. But her body has not been hers since
the beginning of the rainy season."

"God will hear our prayers," I said.

"He holds the knife and He holds the yam."

Because of my position I could see Edna as she came into the middle room. I suppose she must have washed her face with a little water tipped into her palm; she was now wiping it, as she approached us, with a corner of her lappa, which she dropped as soon as she saw me. A big something caught in my throat and I tried without success to swallow it down. She wore a loose blouse over her lappa and an old silken head-tie. As she emerged into the front room all my composure seemed to leave me. Instead of holding out my hand still seated as befitted a man (and one older than she to boot) I sprang to my feet like some woman-fearing Englishman. She screwed up her face ever so slightly in an effort to remember me.

"I am a teacher at the Grammar School," I said a little hoarsely. "We met the day Chief Nanga lectured. . . ."

"Oh yes, it is true," she said smiling gloriously. "You are Mr Samalu."

"That's right," I said, greatly flattered. "You have a good memory on top of your beauty," I said in English so the father would not understand.

"Thank you."

Perhaps it was the way she was dressed and the domestic responsibility she was exercising, or perhaps she had simply grown a little more since October; whatever the reason she was now a beautiful young woman and not a girl looking as though she was waiting to be taken back to her convent.

"Sit down, teacher?" said her father, a little impatiently, I thought. Then turning to his daughter he announced that I had a message from Bori. She turned her largish, round eyes to me.

"Nothing really," I said embarrassed, "Chief Nanga said I should come and greet you and find out about your mother."

"You may tell him she is still in the hospital," said Edna's father in a most unpleasant tone, "and that her medicine costs money and that she planted neither cassava nor cocoyam this year."

"Don't listen to him," said Edna to me, the happiness

wrenched out of her eyes. She turned on her father: "Did he not send you something through his wife?"

"Listen to her," said the man turning to me. "Because she ate yesterday she won't eat today? No, my daughter. This is the time to enjoy an in-law, not when he has claimed his wife and gone away. Our people say: if you fail to take away a strong man's sword when he is on the ground, will you do it when he gets up . . . ? No, my daughter. Leave me and my in-law. He will bring and bring and bring and I will eat until I am tired. And thanks to the Man Above he does not lack what to bring."

"Excuse me," said Edna in English and then explained in our language that she must go and finish her cooking and take lunch to her mother before one o'clock or the nurses would not let her in. She smiled vaguely and turned to go and I had the first opportunity of noticing that her back was as perfect as her front—which happens once in a million. I watched every step she took until she disappeared.

Then I sat on alone with her greedy, avaricious father—for that was the impression I had just formed of him. We said very little. I whistled my silent tune and watched his rope lengthening as he tied one short piece of fibre after another to it. When he had produced a reasonable length he wound it on to the ball.

Edna came into the middle room again and from there asked her father if he had given "the stranger" a kolanut.

"I have none," he said. "If you have, bring it and we will eat."

"I bought some yesterday, I thought I told you." She brought the kolanut in a saucer and gave it to her father who broke the nut after a short avaricious prayer about bringing and eating, threw two lobes into his mouth one after the other, crunched them more noisily than I had ever heard anyone crunch kolanut and passed the saucer to me. I took one of the remaining two and returned the saucer to him.

I sat on and on not knowing what else to do. Should I get up and go? That was hardly sensible. At least I should wait on till Edna came out again even if there was no chance of talking to her privately. Then a wonderful idea struck me. Why not offer to give her a lift on my bicycle to the hospital? It was at least two miles away and my bicycle had a good carrier at the back on which the plates of food could be tied.

"Now that I am here," I told my busy host, "I ought to go and see Edna's mother so that when next I write to Chief Nanga I shall have something to report."

"Don't heed what my daughter says," he told me, looking up from his work. "Tell my in-law that the treatment of his wife's mother is costing me water and firewood."

"I shall certainly say so," I told him. No matter what I might think of him it was clear to me that he was not the kind of man to be bypassed in trying to reach his daughter.

Edna was not in the least surprised by my offer; she was obviously the trusting type—which augured well. I hitched the travelling-can containing the food on to the carrier. I didn't want to ride on the rough approach to the house so I rolled the bicycle the short distance from the house to the road while Edna in a green-and-red floral dress walked beside me. Mounting the vehicle with the can on the back and Edna on the cross-bar proved a little tricky; but I am rather good with bicycles. I solved the problem by getting on the seat first and keeping the bicycle stationary with one foot resting firmly on the ground. Then Edna climbed on the bar sitting sideways; and I pushed off. The excitement of having her so close within my arms and the perfume of her hair in my nose would have proved overpowering if I'd had much time to consider it. I hadn't. The road to the hospital turned out to be quite hilly, not steep but just enough to take the wind out of one; and, with the kind of passenger I had, I didn't care to admit too readily to being tired. So I raced up all the little hillocks until my heart raged like a bonfire, which was very stupid of me.

"You are very strong," said Edna.

"Why?" I said, or rather puffed out, in one enormous expiration, as I rounded the summit of yet another small hill.

"You are eating all the hills like yam."

"I haven't seen any hill yet," I replied, getting back some

of my breath as I pedalled freely down the small, friendly descent that followed. These words were hardly out of my mouth when a stupid sheep and her four or five lambs rushed out of the roadside on my left. I braked sharply. Unfortunately Edna's back was resting on my left arm and prevented me applying the brake on that side effectively. So only the brake on the front wheel performed fully. The bicycle pitched forward and crashed on the road. Just before the impact Edna had cried out something like "My father!" She was thrown farther up the road and as soon as I got up, I rushed to help her to her feet again. Then I turned to gaze at the foofoo and soup in the sandy road. I could have wept. I just stood looking at it and biting my lip. Then Edna burst into nervous laughter which completed my humiliation. I didn't want to look at her. Without taking my eyes from the food I murmured that I was very sorry.

"It was not your fault," she said, "it was the stupid sheep."

Then I noticed with the corner of my eyes that she was bending down. I turned then and saw where she had grazed her knee on the road.

"Oh dear!" I said, "Edna, I am sorry."

She left her frock which she had held up a little at the knee and came to dust my shoulder where my new white shirt carried a thick patch of indelible red-earth. Then she bent down and picked up the travelling-can and began to wipe away the sand, and the spilt soup with green leaves. To my surprise she was crying and saying something like "My mother will die of hunger today". Actually I think her crying was probably due to hurt pride because the food lying on the road showed how poor her family was. But I may be wrong. At the time, however, I was greatly upset.

"Can she manage bread and corned beef?" I asked. "We could buy some outside the hospital."

"I haven't brought any money," said Edna.

"I have some money," I said, feeling the first breath of relief since the accident happened. "And we could get some disinfectant for your knee. I'm terribly sorry, my dear."

10

After the bicycle accident it was clearly impossible to say any of the things I had in mind to Edna. I managed, however, to get out of her that she was going to spend Christmas morning helping Mrs Nanga, and I privately decided to go there myself.

At Christmas the village of Anata, like many other rural communities in our part of the country, always gains in numbers and glamour at the expense of the towns. Its sons and daughters who have gone out to work or trade in the cities usually return home with lots of money to spend. But perhaps the most pleasant gains are the many holidaying students from different secondary schools and training colleges and the very occasional university student. We call them holiday-makers and their presence has a way of immediately raising the general tone of the village, giving it an air of well-dressed sophistication. The boys I saw that morning wore Italian-type shoes and tight trousers and the girls wore lipstick and hair stretched with hot iron; I even saw one in slacks, which I thought was very bold indeed.

When I arrived at Chief Nanga's house at about eleven there was no Edna. Instead a young man whose alcohol-reeking breath hit your nose as soon as you stepped over the threshold was holding forth and telling Mrs Nanga very noisily in pidgin and vernacular to give him a drink. He looked like a trader home from one of the towns. Mrs Nanga was handling him quietly but expertly. She had obviously done this kind of work before. After a year or two's affluence one learned how to handle less fortunate kinsmen.

"Bring me a beer!" the man shouted and hiccupped.

"Honourable Chief Nanga is my brother and he is what white man call V.I.P. . . . Me na P.I.V.—Poor Innocent Victim." He laughed, turning his dopey eyes in my direction. I couldn't help smiling; the wit and inventiveness of our traders is of course world famous.

"Yes, me na P.I.V.," he repeated. "A bottle of beer de cost only five shilling. Chief Honourable Nanga has the money—as of today. Look at the new house he is building. Four storeys! Before, if a man built two storeys the whole town would come to admire it. But today my kinsman is building four. Do I ask to share it with him when it is finished? No. I only ask for common beer, common five shilling beer."

"Why shouldn't you share the house with him?" asked Mrs Nanga deflecting him off his course. "Does a man exclude his brother from his house?"

"No, that is not done," he conceded after thinking about it for a while with his head bent slightly to one side. "It is my house; you have spoken the truth."

The house in question was the very modern four-storey structure going up beside the present building and which was to get into the news later. It was, as we were to learn, a "dash" from the European building firm of Antonio and Sons whom Nanga had recently given the half-million-pound contract to build the National Academy of Arts and Sciences.

I had spent about two hours at the house before Edna finally came in the car sent to bring her. In that time I gave out three shillings to three different groups of boys and their masked dancers. The last, its wooden mask-face a little askew and its stuffed pot-belly looking really stuffed, was held in restraint by his attendants tugging at a rope tied round his waist as adult attendants do to a real, dangerous Mask. The children sang, beat drums, gongs and cigarette cups and the Mask danced comically to the song:

> Sunday, bigi bele Sunday
> Sunday, bigi bele Sunday
> Akatakata done come!
> Everybody run away!
> Sunday, Alleluia!

While the Mask danced here and there brandishing an outsize matchet the restraining rope round his waist came undone. One might have expected this sudden access to freedom to be followed by a wild rampage and loss of life and property. But the Mask tamely put his matchet down, helped his disciples retie the rope, picked up his weapon again and resumed his dance.

When the drunken visitor had finally been persuaded to go and come back later, Mrs Nanga opened a side door that led from the front room into a porch fitted up as a reception room presumably for V.I.P.s and asked me to go in and rest there. Then she sent Edna to me with a bottle of beer and a glass on a tray. She served me silently. But she did not sit down afterwards; instead she went and leaned with her elbows on one of the windows looking outside.

I began to drink the beer and wondered how on earth to begin. I suppose Chief Nanga's house was the wrong place, really. But I had better make the best of it before more visitors came, I thought; and as if to confirm the thought I heard just then the drumming of another group of boys.

"Why don't you sit, Edna?" I said with as much decisiveness as I could put into it.

"I am all right here," she said. "I want to see what is going on in the road."

"Is anything going on?" I stood up and went to her window and was tempted to put an arm round her waist but decided that it might be premature.

"Oh, just people passing in their new Christmas dresses."

"There is something I want to tell you," I said, returning to my seat.

"Me?" she said, turning round and looking genuinely surprised.

"Yes, come and sit down."

She sat down and I took one more sip before speaking.

"I want to give you a piece of advice—as one who has seen more of the world and as a friend." Good beginning, I thought, and took a sip at my glass. "You will be making a big and serious mistake if you allow anyone to rush you into marriage now. You are too young to be rushed into marrying, especially marrying a polygamist. . . ."

"Is that what Mama asked you to tell me?" she asked.

"Who is Mama? Oh, Mrs Nanga, I see. Why? Why should she ask me to tell you anything? No, Edna, it is in your own interest. Don't go and spoil your life."

"What is your business in it?"

"None whatever. Except that I think a beautiful young girl like you deserves better than to marry an ancient polygamist."

"You told my father he was your friend?"

"Even if he was my brother or my father . . . Edna, give yourself a chance. The man's son is almost your age . . ."

"That is the world of women," she said resignedly.

"Rubbish! An educated girl like you saying a thing like that! Are you a Moslem or something?"

She got up from her seat and went back to the window.

"He paid for me to go to the College," she said.

"So what?" I said brusquely and immediately regretted it.

I got up, went to the window and put an arm round her waist. Had my arm been a piece of hot iron she couldn't have reacted more smartly. She swung round and pushed me away in one alarmed movement. We stood thus—maybe four feet apart—looking at each other. Then her eyes fell; she turned again and went back to her window-ledge. I returned to my seat and decided to say nothing more. But the temptation to play the hurt, misunderstood champion was too great.

"I ask your pardon, Edna!" I said. "Do not misunderstand me. You are right that all this is none of my business really. Forget everything I've said."

Hours later, or so it seemed, she replied:

"I am sorry, Odili." And that was the first time she ever used my Christian name. I suppose I should have burst into song, but I didn't.

"Sorry for what?" I said glumly.

"Have I offended you?" she asked with round-eyed, surprised innocence that could have melted a heart of stone. It melted mine.

"How could you offend me?" I asked, not intending the slightest sarcasm.

I was satisfied with the modest progress I seemed to have made. With a girl like Edna what was required was not any precipitous action but a gentle prodding at regular intervals. But while I was making these little private and deliberate decisions in my quiet little corner of Anata, great and momentous events were at last—after long preparation—ready to break and shake all of us out of our leisurely ways.

As the whole world now knows, our Minister of Foreign Trade, Alhaji Chief Senator Suleiman Wagada, announced on New Year's Day a twenty per cent rise in import duties on certain types of textile goods. On January 2nd the Opposition Progressive Alliance Party published detailed evidence to show that someone had told the firm of British Amalgamated of the Minister's plans as long ago as October and that they had taken steps to bring in three shiploads of the textiles by mid-December. The Cabinet was split overnight into the savage warring camps of those who wanted the Government to resign and those, like Chief Nanga, who said that the matter concerned the Minister of Foreign Trade alone and if it came to resigning he should resign by himself. And then the filth began to flow. The *Daily Matchet* for instance carried a story which showed that Chief Nanga, who had himself held the portfolio of Foreign Trade until two years ago, had been guilty of the same practice and had built out of his gains three blocks of seven-storey luxury flats at three hundred thousand pounds each in the name of his wife and that these flats were immediately leased by British Amalgamated at fourteen hundred a month each. At first this and other stories were told in innuendo, but by the second week all restraint and caution were cast to the four winds.

The country was on the verge of chaos. The Trade Unions and the Civil Service Union made loud noises and gave notice of nation-wide strikes. The shops closed for fear of looting. The Governor-General according to rumour called on the Prime Minister to resign which he finally got round to doing three weeks later.

Meanwhile I was summoned to Bori by Max for consultation and to be present at the launching of the C.P.C. We had been caught with only one foot on the ground, so to speak, but we didn't mind in the least. We were exhilarated like everyone else by the heady atmosphere of impending violence. For we all knew that the coming election was going to be a life and death fight. After seven years of lethargy any action seemed welcome and desirable; the country was ripe and impatient to shed in violent exercise the lazy folds of flabby skin and fat it had put on in the greedy years of indolence. The scandals that were daily exposed in the newspapers—far from causing general depression in the country—produced a feeling akin to festivity; I don't mean for people like Chief the Honourable M. A. Nanga, M.P., or Alhaji Chief Senator Suleiman Wagada, but for the rest of us who thought we had nothing to lose.

I returned to Anata with a brand-new Volkswagen, eight hundred pounds in currency notes and assurances that more would be forthcoming. I would have driven straight to see Edna but the shining cream-coloured car was covered in a thick coat of red dust and splattered with brown mud from the long journey, so I decided to go home and have it washed first. Then I drove in style to her place only to be told she had gone to see her grandmother in another village. Her father came out to look at the car, and from the way he did so, you would think he knew a lot about cars. After a very long and thorough inspection he pronounced it a tortoise and chuckled to himself. That visit turned out also to be our last friendly encounter, but I must not anticipate later developments. That was also the day I got home, sat down and composed a very long letter, my first to Edna—giving her all the reasons why she must not marry Chief Nanga.

When I first announced that I was going to contest Chief Nanga's seat everybody laughed—everyone except the wicked outlawed trader, Josiah. He came to me one night out of nowhere and said he would like to join my campaign. I was naturally touched but at the same time knew that having a man with his reputation in our party would be an enormous embarrassment, a sure way to kill the whole thing. So I told him as gently as I could that I had no position to offer him. He stood silent for a while and then told me that I would regret my decision and disappeared again into the night before I had time to tell him to go to hell.

Chief Nanga's constituency (number 136 in the Constituency Register) was made up of five villages including my own home village Urua, and his home-base Anata. I had thought of carrying the battle right to his doorstep by making Anata my headquarters but I soon changed my mind. The inaugural meeting I arranged in the Assembly Hall of the school was completely disrupted at the very last moment by Mr Nwege the Proprietor. A few villagers had come to hear me, or so I thought, and naturally I was furious to find the hall barred. One of the villagers who seemed particularly incensed by the treatment I had received came forward to introduce himself, or so it seemed to me.

"So you are Mr Samalu?" he said. "Pleased to meet you." There was a lot of fellow feeling on his face.

I stretched my hand to take his. But instead of a handshake

he smartly described an arc at my head and knocked off my
red cap. The small crowd thought it was very funny and
laughed boisterously. I decided to remain cool and dignified; I
bent down to pick up my cap and to my greatest shock and
mortification the rascal kicked me behind—not violently but
enough to make me land on my two hands, to avoid landing
on my head. I was ready for a fight then but the cowardly fellow had taken to his heels—to the applause of most of the
people around, the very people I had assumed came to hear
me. I decided there and then that I was in hostile territory and
must recruit a bodyguard and move to my own village. But
Anata had not finished with me yet. That night Mr Nwege
sent a boy to call me. When I got to his "Lodge" he handed me
a month's salary and a notice of dismissal. I was about to thank
him for so obligingly setting fire to a house that was due for
demolition and saving someone's labour, when he snarled:

"I see that you have grown too big for your coat." My
thanks died in my throat.

"You have grown too small in yours, Mr Push-me-down," I
said instead, laughing boisterously in his amazed face. It was
an enormous release for me after all the pent-up annoyance of
that afternoon. "Yes, Mr Push-me-down, you have shrivelled
up in your coat."

He sprang up from his seat and I thought (or hoped) he was
coming to assault me. But no; rather he rushed into an inner
room probably to get his double-barrelled gun or something. I
didn't wait to find out.

It was now four days since I had returned from Bori and I
had not seen Mrs Nanga yet, nor Edna for that matter. And
that was going to be my last working day—so to speak—
before I moved my headquarters to Urua.

Frankly I had no more business to do with Mrs Nanga. But
a sort of conspiratorial friendship had sprung up between us
and I would have felt very bad not to have said good-bye to
her. There was also a dash of plain curiosity in it; I wanted to
know how she was taking the news that I was contesting her
husband's seat. At that point I was still naïve enough in my

political thinking to have that kind of curiosity. But perhaps my strongest reason for going was the odd chance of seeing Edna there.

The front door was open and I walked in clapping my hands.

"Who?" asked Mrs Nanga from somewhere inside.

"Me," I said at the top of my voice.

"There is a seat," she called out.

I sat down facing the approaches to the house. Soon I heard her coming, her slippers clapping against the soles of her feet; and she was humming a tune.

I turned my head and our faces met. She stopped dead at the doorway.

"Good morning, Mrs Nanga," I said.

"What do you want here?" Her Adam's apple was agitated by a hard swallowing.

"I only come to say good-bye," I said, getting up.

"I do not need your good-bye, do you hear me? And you may thank your personal spirit that there is no strong man in the house. That is why you can sneak here in the noonday. . . ."

"Pardon me—" I began, but was not allowed to finish.

Mrs Nanga had suddenly and dramatically raised her voice so the entire village could hear and was calling on all the gods of her people to come and witness that she was sitting in her house, as a weak person was wont to sit when her tormentor, to show how strong he was, brought a fight to her very door-step. . . . I heard most of this recitative on my way to the car. I had begun the retreat as soon as she had removed her head-tie and girdled her waist firmly with it pulling the two ends as I had seen Edna's father pull his rope.

As it was nearly midday I drove from Mrs Nanga's house to the Anata Mission Hospital to waylay Edna. After more than an hour in my car I did what I should have done in the first place. I decided to go to the Women's ward. But the gateman refused to let my car through. I didn't mind that but I certainly minded his rudeness—and told him so. All he had to do was tell me politely that cars were not allowed in the hospital unless they were carrying a patient. Instead he shouted at me like a mad dog and said, pointing at the notice:

"Abi you no fit read notice?"

"Don't be silly," I said, "and don't shout at me!"

"Be silly!" he shouted. "Idiot like you. Look him motor self. When they call those wey get motor you go follow them co-mot? Foolish idiot."

I parked my car outside the gate and went in, deciding to ignore the man who had not ceased shouting.

"Na him make accident de kill them for road every day. Nonsense!"

As I approached the wards the man's shrill voice rang in my ear pronouncing one evil wish after another. I reflected on the depth of resentment and hatred from which such venom came—and for no other reason than that I owned a car, or seemed to own one! It was depressing and quite frightening. And when I got to the ward and was told with pointless brusqueness by a girl-nurse that my patient had been discharged yesterday I felt really downcast. As a rule I don't like suffering to no purpose. Suffering should be creative, should give birth to something good and lovely. So I drove from the hospital to Edna's place, although her father had told me three days earlier never to set foot in his house again. And for the first time since my return from Bori my luck was on. Edna was in and her father was out. But apparently he had only gone behind the compound—presumably to ease himself. Edna pleaded with me to go.

"No," I said.

"He will kill you if he finds you here."

"That would be wonderful," I said in English.

"I will come to your place to see you if you go now."

"You can't because I leave Anata tomorrow morning. I have been dismissed from the school. How is your mother? I've just been to the hospital to see her."

Edna's eyes darted from me to the door of the middle room, from which I imagined her father would appear, and darted back again. She was literally shaking with fear. Somehow I was enjoying her terror. It was as though I was drunk—with what I couldn't say.

"Please, Odili," she said again, with tears in her voice.

"Say 'please, Odili' one hundred times and I shall go," I said, throwing my limbs in all directions for relaxation.

"Oh, you think it is a laughing matter. All right, sit there."

She sat down on the other hard chair and folded her arms under her perfectly formed breasts.

"Please, Odili," she said, getting up again quickly and wringing her hands.

"One!"

"What is all this?" she said in despair.

"Minus one."

At that moment her father cleared his throat inside the compound. She grabbed my arm and tried to pull me up. I laughed at her puny effort and settled back. Her father had now come into the house and we could hear his footsteps.

"You see now. . . . What is all this?"

He took a little time to focus his eyes properly and decide who I was. When he had decided he took a few more steps until he stood threateningly over me.

"Who do you want here?" he asked with menacing quietness. "Were you not the one I told the other day never to come here again?"

"Yes," I said, not even bothering to get up.

"Wait for me," he said, and rushed back the way he had come. Lately I had seen too many people rushing around threateningly, so that I decided to sit through this one. I wasn't even touched by Edna's weeping. She turned and ran, calling "Mother! Mother!" But at the door she met her father who shoved her aside and came at me with a raised matchet.

I said: "Who do you want here?"

Edna increased her crying which finally brought her sick mother unsteadily to the doorway. Meanwhile I was explaining to my assailant that I came to persuade him and his family to cast their paper for me on voting day.

"Do you think the boy's head is correct?" he asked of no

one in particular, and I saw his matchet gradually descend to his side. By the time Edna's mother appeared the worst of the danger seemed over.

"That is the boy who brought me bread, is it not?" she asked as she tottered towards me holding out a shrunken, varicose hand.

"I don't care what he brought you," said her husband. "What I know is that he is poking his finger into my in-law's eyes."

"How?" asked the woman, and her husband explained. She listened carefully, thought about it and then said:

"What is my share in that? They are both white man's people. And they know what is what between themselves. What do we know?"

Before I left the place an hour or so later, Edna's father had given me a sound piece of advice—at least sound in his own eyes.

"My in-law is like a bull," he said, "and your challenge is like the challenge of a tick to a bull. The tick fills its belly with blood from the back of the bull and the bull doesn't even know it's there. He carries it wherever he goes—to eat, drink or pass ordure. Then one day the cattle egret comes, perches on the bull's back and picks out the tick. . . ."

"Thank you very much for your advice," I said.

"I hear that they have given you much money to use in fighting my in-law," he continued. "If you have sense in your belly you will carry the money into your bed-chamber and stow it away and do something useful with it. It is your own good luck. But if you prefer to throw it away why not ask me to help you?"

It was amazing how quickly all kinds of rumour about my plans had spread. It usually took a telegram five days to get to this village from Bori—that is, provided the Post and Telegraph boys were not on strike, and a storm had not felled tree branches across telegraph wires anywhere along the three-hundred-mile route. But a rumour could generally make it in one day or less.

When I rose to go, Edna, who had kept very much in the background during the last hour, rose to see me off to the car.

"Where are you going?" asked her father.

"To see him off."

"To see whom off? Don't let me lay hands on you this afternoon."

"Bye, bye," she said from the doorway.

"Bye," I said, trying to smile.

11

As I drove away thinking of the courage and indifference to personal danger I had just shown, I felt a tingling glow of satisfaction spread all over me as palm-oil does on hot yam. Also the way Edna had looked at me when she said "bye, bye" showed plainly that my fearlessness had not been lost on her either. And at that very moment I was suddenly confronted by a fact I had been dodging for some time. I knew then that I wanted Edna now (if not all along) for her own sake first and foremost and only very remotely as part of a general scheme of revenge. I had started off telling myself that I was going for her in order to hurt Chief Nanga; now I would gladly chop off Chief Nanga's head so as to get her. Funny, wasn't it? Having got that far in my self-analysis I had to ask myself one question. How important was my political activity in its own right? It was difficult to say; things seemed so mixed up; my revenge, my new political ambition and the girl. And perhaps it was just as well that my motives should entangle and reinforce one another. For I was not being so naïve as to imagine that loving Edna was enough to wrench her from a minister. True, I had other advantages like youth and education but those were nothing beside wealth and position and the authority of a greedy father. No. I needed all the reinforcement I could get. Although I had little hope of winning Chief Nanga's seat, it was necessary nonetheless to fight and expose him as much as possible so that, even if he won, the Prime Minister would find it impossible to re-appoint him to his Cabinet. In fact there was already enough filth clinging to his name to disqualify him—and most of his colleagues as well—but we are not as strict as some countries. That is why C.P.C. publicity had to ferret out every scandal and blow it up, and maybe someone would get up and say: "No, Nanga has taken more than the owner could ignore!" But it was no more than a hope.

As I drove down the very same incline on which Edna and I had so dramatically come to grief over a black sheep and its lambs only a few weeks earlier, I could not help thinking also of the quick transformations that were such a feature of our country, and in particular of the changes of attitude in my own self. I had gone to the University with the clear intention of coming out again after three years as a full member of the privileged class whose symbol was the car. So much did I think of it in fact that, as early as my second year, I had gone and taken out a driver's licence and even made a mental note of the make of car I would buy. (It had a gadget which turned the seats into a bed in a matter of seconds.) But in my final year I had passed through what I might call a period of intellectual crisis brought on partly by my radical Irish lecturer in history and partly by someone who five years earlier had been by all accounts a fire-eating president of our Students' Union. He was now an ice-cream-eating Permanent Secretary in the Ministry of Labour and Production and had not only become one of the wealthiest and most corrupt landlords in Bori but was reported in the Press as saying that trade-union leaders should be put in detention. He became for us a classic example of the corroding effect of privilege. We burnt his effigy on the floor of the Union Building from which he had made fine speeches against the Government, and were fined by the University authorities for blacking the ceiling. Many of us vowed then never to be corrupted by bourgeois privileges of which the car was the most visible symbol in our country. And now here was I in this marvellous little affair eating the hills like yam—as Edna would have said. I hoped I was safe; for a man who avoids danger for years and then gets killed in the end has wasted his care.

As soon as I got home, my boy Peter handed me a blue envelope. The writing was beautifully rounded; without doubt a woman's hand. It wasn't Joy's (Joy was a casual friend teaching in a near-by school); I hoped with a pounding heart that it was from Edna. But it couldn't be, she would have said something about it when I saw her an hour or so ago.

"A boy brought it on a bicycle. Soon after you left in the morning," said Peter.

"All right," I said. "Go away."

I tried to open it fast and then held back for fear of what it might contain. Also I didn't want to destroy the beautiful envelope. It *was* Edna! Why hadn't she mentioned it?

Dear Odili,

Your missive of 10th instant was received and its contents well noted. I cannot adequately express my deep sense of gratitude for your brotherly pieces of advice. It is just a pity that you did not meet me in the house when you came last time. My brother has narrated to me how my father addressed you badly and disgraced you. I am really sorry about the whole episode and I feel like going on a bended knee to beg forgiveness. I know that you are so noble and kind-hearted to forgive me before even I ask [smiles!].

I have noted carefully all what you said about my marriage. Really, you should pity poor me, Odili. I am in a jam about the whole thing. If I develop cold feet now my father will almost kill me. Where is he going to find all the money the man has paid on my head? So it is not so much that I want to be called a minister's wife but a matter of can't help. What cannot be avoided must be borne.

What I pray for is happiness. If God says that I will be happy in any man's house I will be happy.

I hope we will always be friends. For yesterday is but a dream and

tomorrow is only a vision but today's friendship makes every yesterday a dream
of happiness and every tomorrow a vision of hope.

Good-bye and sweet dreams.

Yours v. truly,

Edna Odo

P.S. My brother told me you have bought a new car. Congrats and more grease
to your elbows. I hope you will carry me in it one day in remembrance of the
bicycle accident [smiles!].

Edna.

It was dated yesterday. She must have been expecting me to
mention it, or perhaps she was too concerned about my safety.

I read it again standing up, then sitting down and finally
lying on the bed, flat on my back. Some of it was Edna and
some (like the bit about visions of tomorrow) clearly was not; it
must have come straight from one of these so-called "Letter
Writers". I remember one—*The Complete Loveletter Writer*—
which was very popular with us in my school days. It was written, printed and published by an adventurous trader in Kataki
and claimed on its front cover to have sold 500,000 copies,
which I believe was merely a way of saying that it had sold a
few hundred copies or hoped to do so. I know some foreigners
think we are funny with figures. One day when I was still at
the University, an old District Officer with whom my father
had worked long ago came to our house; he had just come back
to our area as adviser on co-operatives after years of retirement
and was paying a call on his old interpreter. As they talked in
the parlour my younger half-brothers and sisters kept up an
endless procession in front of the strange visitor until he was
constrained to ask my father how many children he had.

"About fifteen," said my father.

"About? Surely you must know."

My father grinned and talked about other things. Of course
he knew how many children he had but people don't go count-
ing their children as they do animals or yams. And the same I
fear goes for our country's population.

But to return to Edna's letter. Having mentally removed

those parts of it which were not her sweet spontaneous self I began to analyse the rest word by word to try and discover how I stood in her estimation. First of all "Dear Odili" was somewhat disappointing; I had written "My dearest Edna" in my own letter and if interest was mutual the correct way would be for the woman to reply in the same degree of fondness or perhaps one grade lower—which in this case would be "My dear Odili". Anyway there were small compensations dotted here and there in the main body of the letter and I was prepared to place considerable weight on "sweet dreams". Altogether I felt a little encouraged to launch my offensive against Chief Nanga.

As soon as I returned to my own village I set about organizing my bodyguard. There were four of them, and their leader was a tough called Boniface who had arrived in our village a few years before from no one knew where. He didn't even speak our language at the time. He does now, but still prefers pidgin. I don't know whether it is true that he had a single bone in his forearm instead of the normal two but that was the story. He sometimes behaved like a crazy man which he himself admitted openly, saying it had arisen from a boyhood accident in which he fell down a mango tree and landed on his head. I paid him ten pounds a month and gave him food, which was quite generous; his three assistants earned much less. Wherever I went in my campaigning, Boniface sat with me in front and the other three at the back of the car. As our journeys became more and more hazardous I agreed to our carrying the minimum of weapons strictly for defence. We had five matchets, a few empty bottles and stones in the boot. Later we were compelled to add two double-barrelled guns. I only agreed to this most reluctantly after many acts of violence were staged against us, like the unprovoked attack by some hoodlums and thugs calling themselves Nanga's Youth Vanguard or Nangavanga, for short. New branches of this Nangavanga were springing up every day throughout the district. Their declared aim was to "annihilate all enemies of progress" and "to project true Nangaism". The fellows we ran into carried placards, one of which read:

NANGAISM FOREVER: SAMALU IS TREITOR. It was the first time I had seen myself on a placard and I felt oddly elated. It was also amusing, really, how the cowards slunk away from the roadblocks they had put up when Boniface reached out and grabbed two of their leaders, brought their heads together like dumb-bells and left them to fall to either side of him. You should have seen them fall like cut banana trunks. It was then I acquired my first trophy—the placard with my name on it. But I lost my windscreen which they smashed with stones. It was funny but from then on I began to look out for unfriendly placards carrying my name and to feel somewhat disappointed if I didn't see them or saw too few.

One early morning Boniface and one of the other stalwarts woke me up and demanded twenty-five pounds. I knew that a certain amount of exploitation was inevitable in this business and I wasn't going to question how every penny was spent. But at the same time I didn't see how I could abdicate my responsibility for C.P.C. funds entrusted to me. I had to satisfy my conscience that I was exercising adequate control.

"I gave you ten pounds only yesterday," I said and was about to add that unlike our opponents we had very limited funds—a point which I had already made many times. But Boniface interrupted me.

"Are you there?" he said. "If na play we de play make you tell us because me I no wan waste my time for nothing sake. Or you think say na so so talk talk you go take win Chief Nanga. If Government no give you plenty money for election make you go tell them no be sand sand we de take do am. . . ."

"Man no fit fight tiger with empty hand," added his companion before I could put in a word to correct Boniface's fantastic misconception.

"No be Government de give us money," I said. "We na small party, C.P.C. We wan help poor people like you. How Government go give us money . . . ?"

"But na who de give the er weting call . . . P.C.P. money?" asked Boniface puzzled.

"Some friends abroad," I said with a knowing air to cover my own ignorance which I had forgotten to worry about in the heat of activity.

"You no fit send your friends telegram?" asked Boniface's companion.

"Let's not go into that now. What do you need twenty-five pounds for? And what have you done with the ten pounds?" I felt I had to sound firm. It worked.

"We give three pound ten to that policeman so that he go spoil the paper for our case. Then we give one-ten to Court Clerk because they say as the matter done reach him eye the policeman no kuku spoil am just like that. Then we give another two pound . . ."

"All right," I said. "What do you want the twenty-five pounds for?"

"They no tell you say Chief Nanga done return back from Bori yesterday?"

"So you wan give am money too?" I asked.

"This no be matter for joke; we wan the money to pay certain porsons wey go go him house for night and burn him car."

"What! No, we don't need to do that." There was a minute's silence.

"Look my frien' I done tell you say if you no wan serious for this business make you go rest for house. I done see say you want play too much gentleman for this matter . . . Dem tell you say na gentlemanity de give other people minister . . . ? Anyway wetin be my concern there? Na you sabi."

My father's attitude to my political activity intrigued me a lot. He was, as I think I have already indicated, the local chairman of P.O.P. in our village, Urua, and so I expected that his house would not contain both of us. But I was quite wrong. He took the view (without expressing it in so many words) that the mainspring of political action was personal gain, a view which, I might say, was much more in line with

the general feeling in the country than the high-minded thinking of fellows like Max and I. The only comment I remember
my father making (at the beginning anyway) was when he
asked if my "new" party was ready to give me enough money to
fight Nanga. He sounded a little doubtful. But he was clearly
satisfied with what I had got out of it so far, especially the car
which he was now using nearly as much as myself. The normal
hostility between us was put away in a corner, out of sight. But
very soon all that was to change, and then change again.

We were sitting in his outbuilding one day about noon
reading yesterday's newspapers which I had just bought from
the local newsagent and hairdresser, Jolly Barber, when I saw
Chief Nanga's Cadillac approaching. I thought of going into
the main house but decided against it. After all, he was walk-
ing into my own lair and if anyone was to feel flustered it
shouldn't be me but the intruder. I told my father who was
peering helplessly at the car that it was Chief Nanga and he
immediately reached for a singlet to cover the upper part of his
body, re-tied his enormous lappa nervously and went to the
doorstep to receive the visitor wearing a flabby, ingratiating
smile—the type our people describe so aptly as putrid. I sat
where I was, pretending to read.

"Hello! Odili, my great enemy," greeted Chief Nanga in
the most daring assault of counterfeit affability I had ever seen
or thought possible.

"Hello," I said as flat as the floor.

"Did you see Chief the Honourable Minister yesterday?"
asked my father severely.

"Let him be, sir," said Chief Nanga. "He and I like to say
harsh things to each other in jest. Those who don't know us
may think we are about to cut off one another's heads . . ."

I settled farther back in my cane chair and raised the newspaper higher. He tried a few more times to draw me out but I
stoutly refused to open my mouth, even when my father foolishly shouted at me and drew near as though to strike me.
Fortunately for both of us he didn't do it; for me it would
have spelled immediate disaster; a man who hit his father

wouldn't have had much of a hearing thereafter in my constituency. It was interesting to me—thinking about it later—how Chief Nanga who had been so loudly interceding for me (or appearing to do so) suddenly withdrew into expectant silence, praying no doubt that my father's rage would push him over the brink. When he realized that his prayer would not be answered after all he said, without the slightest hint of falseness, "Don't worry about Odili, sir. If a young man does not behave like a young man who is going to?"

"He should wait till he builds his own house then he may put his head into a pot there—not here in my house. If he has no respect for me why should he carry his foolishness to such an important guest . . . ?"

"Never mind, sir. I am no guest here. I regard here as my house and yourself as my political father. Whatever we achieve over there in Bori is because we have the backing of people like you at home. All these young boys who are saying all kinds of rubbish against me, what do they know? They hear that Chief Nanga has eaten ten per cent commission and they begin to break their heads and holler up and down. They don't know that all the commissions are paid into party funds. . . ."

I had lowered my newspaper to half-mast, so to speak.

"That's right," said my father knowingly, but I could tell by watching his face that his final state of knowledge was achieved through an effort of will. At first he had seemed puzzled by Nanga's explanation and then I suppose he felt that as a local chairman of P.O.P. he could not admit to ignorance of its affairs so he immediately knew. As in breaking the law, what one knows and what one ought to know come to the same thing.

"I suppose your new four-storeyed building is going to be the party headquarters," I asked, putting down the newspaper altogether.

"Chief the Honourable Minister was not talking to you," said my father lamely.

"Naturally he wouldn't because he knows I know what he

knows . . . The buses, for instance, we all know are for carrying the party, and the import duty . . ."

"Shut up!" shouted my father.

"Leave him alone, sir. When he finishes advertising his ignorance I will educate him."

I wanted to say he should go and educate his mother but decided against it.

"Have you finished, Mr Nationalist? He that knows not and knows not that he knows not is a fool."

"Don't mind him, Chief. He is my son but I can tell you that if I had another like him I would have died long ago. Let us go into the house." My father led the way to the dark parlour of the main house—a stone and cement building which was once the best and most modern house in Urua. But today nobody remembers it when buildings are talked about. It has become old-fashioned with its high, steep roof into which had gone enough corrugated iron sheets for at least two other houses. Some day someone will have to replace the wooden jalousie of its narrow windows with glass panes so as to let in more light into the rooms. And most likely the someone will be me.

I stayed on in the outbuilding exulting in my successful onslaught which had driven my father and his important guest from this airy comfortable day-room into the dark stone house.

About half an hour later my father came to the front door of the main house and called my name. "Sir!" I answered full of respect but without getting up or stirring in any way.

"Come in here," he said. I took my time to get up and walk over. A bottle of whisky and another of soda stood on a tray on the small round table in the middle of the room. Chief Nanga's glass was half full; my father's empty, as usual.

"Sit down," he said to me; "we don't eat people." The joviality in his tone and manner put me on guard right away.

I sat down ostentatiously ignoring to look in Nanga's direction. My father didn't waste his words.

"When a mad man walks naked it is his kinsmen who feel shame not himself. So I have been begging Chief Nanga for forgiveness, on your behalf. How could you go to his house asking for his help and eating his food and then spitting in his face? . . . Let me finish. You did not tell me any of these things—that you abused him in public and left his house to plot his downfall. . . . I said let me finish! It does not surprise me that you slunk back and said nothing about it to me. Not that you ever say anything to me. Why should you? Do I know book? Am I not of the Old Testament? . . . Let me finish. In spite of your behaviour Chief Nanga has continued to struggle for you and has now brought you the scholarship to your house. His kindness surprises me; I couldn't do it myself. On top of that he has brought you two hundred and fifty pounds if you will sign this paper. . . ." He held up a piece of paper.

"Don't say I am interrupting you, sir," said Chief Nanga. "I don't want Odili to misunderstand me." He turned squarely to me. "I am not afraid of you. Every goat and every fowl in this country knows that you will fail woefully. You will lose your deposit and disgrace yourself. I am only giving you this money because I feel that after all my years of service to my people I deserve to be elected unopposed so that my detractors in Bori will know that I have my people solidly behind me.

"That is the only reason I am giving you this money. Otherwise I should leave you alone to learn your bitter lesson so that when you hear of election again you will run. . . . I know those irresponsible boys have given you money. If you have any sense keep the money and train your father's children with it or do something useful. . . ."

I stayed miraculously unruffled. Actually I was thinking about Edna all along. But I noticed also how my father had raised his nose in the air in proud rejection of the offer I hadn't made—nor intended to make—to train his children.

"We know where that money is coming from," continued Nanga. "Don't think we don't know. We will deal with them after the election. They think they can come here and give money to irresponsible people to overthrow a duly consti-tuted government. We will show them. As for you my brother you can eat what has entered your hand. . . . Your good friend Maxwell Kulamo has more sense than you. He has already taken his money and agreed to step down for Chief Koko."

"Impossible!"

"Look at him. He doesn't even know what is happening; our great politician! You stay in the bush here wasting your time and your friends are busy putting their money in the bank in Bori. Anyway you are not a small boy. I have done my best and, God so good, your father is my living witness. Take your money and take your scholarship to go and learn more book; the country needs experts like you. And leave the dirty game of politics to us who know how to play it . . ."

"Do you want an answer? It is NO in capital letters! You think everyone can be bought with a few dirty pounds. You're making a sad mistake. I will fight you along the road and in the bush, even if you buy the entire C.P.C. I can see you are trying to cover your fear. I see the fear in your eyes. If you know you are not afraid why do you send thugs to molest me; why do your hired cowards carry placards with my name. I am sorry, Mr Man, you can take your filthy money away and clear out of here . . . Bush man!"

"Odili!"

It was I who had to clear out there and then. As I passed by the Cadillac I noticed four or five thugs in it, one of whom looked familiar although I did not get close enough to see them well.

I knew it was a lie about Max agreeing to step down but I began to wonder why he hadn't arrived yet to mount our campaign in my constituency.

12

"A mad man may sometimes speak a true word," said my father, "but, you watch him, he will soon add something to it that will tell you his mind is still spoilt. My son, you have again shown your true self. When you came home with a car I thought to myself: good, some sense is entering his belly at last . . . But I should have known. So you really want to fight Chief Nanga! My son, why don't you fall where your pieces could be gathered? If the money he was offering was too small why did you not say so? Why did you not ask for three or four hundred? But then your name would not be Odili if you did that. No, you have to insult the man who came to you as a friend and—let me ask you something: Do you think he will return tomorrow to beg you again with two-fifty pounds? No, my son. You have lost the sky and you have lost the ground. . . ."

"Why do you worry yourself and get lean over a loss that

is mine and not yours at all? You are in P.O.P. and I am in C.P.C. . . ."

"You have to listen to my irritating voice until the day comes when you stop answering Odili Samalu or else until you look for me and don't see me any more."

This softened me a lot. I am always sentimental when it comes to people not being seen when they are looked for. I said nothing immediately but when I did it was in a more conciliatory tone.

"So your party gives ministers authority to take bribes, eh?"

"What?" he said, waking up. I hadn't been looking at him and so didn't notice when he had dropped off.

"Chief Nanga said that the ten per cent he receives on contracts is for your party. Is that true?"

"If Alligator comes out of the water one morning and tells you that Crocodile is sick can you doubt his story?"

"I see." This time I watched him drop off almost immediately and smiled in spite of myself.

The next day Max and our campaign team arrived from Bori. There were a dozen other people with him, only two of whom I knew already—Eunice his fiancée and the trade-unionist, Joe. They had a car, a minibus and two brand-new Land-Rovers with loudspeakers fitted on the roof. Seeing them so confident and so well-equipped was for me the most morale-boosting event of the past so many weeks. I envied Max his beautiful, dedicated girl; some people are simply lucky. I wished I could bring Edna there to see them.

"You didn't tell me you were coming today," I said to Max; "not that it matters."

"Didn't you get my telegram?"

"No."

"I sent you a telegram on Monday."

"Monday of this week? Oh well, today is only Thursday; it should get here on Saturday . . ."

"D.V.," said Max.

Everyone laughed as I led them to my father's outbuilding. He had on seeing them quickly put on his browning singlet and was now shaking hands with everyone with as much enthusiasm as if he had been our patron. My young brothers and sisters were all over the place, some making faces at their image on the shining car bodies. The cars must have been washed at the ferry, I thought. It was typical of Max to want to come in clean and spotless. Two or three of my father's wives came to the door of the inner compound and called out greetings to the visitors. Then Mama, the senior wife, came out hurriedly clutching a telegram.

"It came this morning while you were out; I just remembered it," she said to me. "I told Edmund to remind me as soon as you returned, but the foolish boy . . ."

Everyone laughed again and my father catching the hilarity terminated the rebuke he had begun to deliver to "those who can't read but love to handle other people's letters . . ."

"We must withdraw our earlier statements," said Max, "and give three hearty cheers to the Ministry of Posts and Telegraphs.

"Hip, hip-hip———"

"Hurrah!"

"HIP, HIP, HIP———"

"Hurrah!"

"For they are jolly good fellows
For they are jolly good fellows
For they are jolly good fellows
And so say all of us.
And so say all of us, hurrah!
And so say all of us, hurrah!
For they are jolly good fellows
For they are jolly good fellows
For they are jolly good fellows
And so say all of us."

The singing and the laughter and the sight of so many cars brought in neighbours and passers-by until we had a small crowd.

"Why don't we launch our campaign here and now?" asked Max with glazed intoxicated-looking eyes.

"Why not indeed?" said Eunice.

"Not here," I said firmly. "My father is local chairman of P.O.P. and we shouldn't embarrass him . . . In any case people don't launch campaigns just like that on the spur of the moment."

"What is the boy talking?" asked my father. "What has my being in P.O.P. got to do with it? I believe that the hawk should perch and the eagle perch, whichever says to the other *don't,* may its own wing break."

My comrades applauded him and sang "For he is a jolly good fellow" again. This time the loudspeakers had been switched on and the entire neighbourhood rang with song. By the time four or five highlife records had been played as well, the compound became too small for our audience. Every chair and kitchen-stool in the house was brought out and arranged in a half-moon for the elders and village dignitaries. A microphone was set up on the steps of the outbuilding facing the crowd. What impressed them right away was how you could talk into that ball and get the voice thundering in a completely different place. "Say what you will," I heard someone remark, "the white man is a spirit."

Max's unprepared speech—or perhaps it was prepared in its broad outlines—was on the whole impressive. But I do not think that it persuaded many people. Actually it wasn't a speech in the strict sense but a dialogue between him and the audience, or a vociferous fraction of the audience. There was one man who proved particularly troublesome. He had been a police corporal who had served two years in jail for corruptly receiving ten shillings from a lorry driver. That was the official version anyway. The man's own story was that he had been framed because he had stood up against his white boss in pre-Independence days. I believe there was a third version which put the blame on enemies from another tribe. Whatever the true story, on his release, "Couple", as the villagers still called him, had come back to his people and become a local councillor and politician. He was at the moment very much involved in supplying stones for our village pipe-borne water scheme and was widely accused (in whispers) of selling one heap of stones in the morning, carrying it away at night and selling it again the next day; and repeating the cycle as long as he liked. He was of course in league with the Local Council Treasurer.

Max began by accusing the outgoing Government of all kinds of swindling and corruption. As he gave instance after instance of how some of our leaders who were ash-mouthed paupers five years ago had become near-millionaires under our very eyes, many in the audience laughed. But it was the laughter of resignation to misfortune. No one among them swore vengeance; no one shook with rage or showed any sign of fight. They understood what was being said, they had seen it with their own eyes. But what did anyone expect them to do?

The ex-policeman put it very well. "We know they are eating," he said, "but we are eating too. They are bringing us water and they promise to bring us electricity. We did not have those things before; that is why I say we are eating too."

"Defend them, Couple," cried someone in the audience to him. "Are you not one of them when it comes to eating aged guinea-fowls?"

This brought a good deal of laughter but again it was a slack, resigned laughter. No one seemed ready to follow up the reprimand or join issue with Couple for defending his fellow racketeers.

Up to this point Max had spoken slowly and deliberately, with very little heat. But now, as he accused the present regime of trying to establish itself as a privileged class sitting on the back of the rest of us, his hands and his voice began to shake.

"Whether it is P.O.P. or P.A.P. they are the same," he cried.

"The same ten and ten pence," agreed someone in English.

"They want to share out the wealth of the country between them. That is why you must reject both; that is why we have now formed the C.P.C. as a party of the ordinary people like yourselves. . . . Once upon a time a hunter killed some big-game at night. He searched for it in vain and at last he decided to go home and await daylight. At the first light of morning he returned to the forest full of expectation. And what do you think he found? He saw two vultures fighting over what still remained of the carcass. In great anger he loaded his gun and shot the two dirty uneatable birds. You may say that he was foolish to waste his bullet on them but I say no. He was angry and he wanted to wipe out the dirty thieves fighting over another man's inheritance. That hunter is yourselves. Yes, you and you and you. And the two vultures—P.O.P. and P.A.P. . . ." There was loud applause. Jolly good, I thought.

"There were three vultures," said the ex-policeman after the applause had subsided. "The third and youngest was called C.P.C."

"Why don't you leave the young man alone to tell us his story?" asked one elderly woman smoking a short clay pipe. But many people obviously thought the ex-policeman very witty and I saw one or two shaking his hand.

Towards the end of his speech Max made one point which frankly I thought unworthy of him or of C.P.C. but I suppose I am too finicky. "We all know," he said, "what one dog said to another. He said: 'If I fall for you this time and you fall for me next time then I know it is play not fight.' Last time you elected a Member of Parliament from Anata. Now it is your turn here in Urua. A goat does not eat into a hen's stomach no matter how friendly the two may be. Ours is ours but mine is mine. I present as my party's candidate your own son, Odili Samalu . . ." He walked over to me and held my hand up and the crowd cheered and cheered.

An elderly man who I believe was also a local councillor now stood up. He had sat on the edge of his seat directly opposite the microphone, his two hands like a climber's grasping his iron staff. His attitude and posture had shown total absorption in what was being said:

"I want to thank the young man for his beautiful words," he said. "Every one of them has entered my ear. I always say that what is important nowadays is no longer age or title but knowledge. The young man clearly has it and I salute him.

There is one word he said which entered my ear more than everything else—not only entered but built a house there. I don't know whether you others heard it in the same way as I did. That word was that our own son should go and bring our share." There was great applause from the crowd. "That word entered my ear. The village of Anata has already eaten, now they must make way for us to reach the plate. No man in Urua will give his paper to a stranger when his own son needs it; if the very herb we go to seek in the forest now grows at our very back yard are we not saved the journey? We are ignorant people and we are like children. But I want to tell our son one thing: He already knows where to go and what to say when he gets there; he should tell them that we are waiting here like a babe cutting its first tooth: anyone who wants to look at our new tooth should know that his bag should be heavy. Have I spoken well?"

"Yes," answered the crowd as they began to disperse.

Later I called Max aside and told him excitedly and in a few words about Chief Nanga's visit.

"You should have taken the money from him," he replied.

"What?" I was thunderstruck.

"Chief Koko offered me one thousand pounds," he continued placidly. "I consulted the other boys and we decided to accept. It paid for that minibus . . ."

"I don't understand you, Max. Are you telling me that you have taken money and stepped down for P.O.P.?"

"I am telling you nothing of the sort. The paper I signed has no legal force whatever and we needed the money . . ."

"It had moral force," I said, downcast. "I am sorry, Max, but I think you have committed a big blunder. I thought we wanted our fight to be clean . . . You had better look out; they will be even more vicious from now on and people will say they have cause." I was really worried. If our people understand nothing else they know that a man who takes money from another in return for service must render that service or remain vulnerable to that man's just revenge. Neither God nor juju would save him.

"Oh, forget that. Do you know, Odili, that British Amalgamated has paid out four hundred thousand pounds to P.O.P. to fight this election? Yes, and we also know that the Americans have been even more generous, although we don't have the figures as yet. Now you tell me how you propose to fight such a dirty war without soiling your hands a little. Just you tell me. Anyway we must be moving on to Abaga now. I'll be here again in a couple of days to iron out everything and let you know our detailed plans from now on. Meanwhile, old boy, if the offer comes again take it. It's as much your money as his . . ."

"Never!"

"Anyway, the question is purely academic now . . . Your old man is a wonderful fellow. I like him."

Seeing Max and Eunice once again, sharing every excitement, had made my mouth water, to put it crudely. As Max made his speech I had found myself watching Eunice's beautiful profile. She sat at the edge of her chair, wringing her clasped hands like a nervous schoolgirl. Her lips seemed to be forming the same words that he was uttering. Perhaps it was this delicious picture of feminine loyalty that led me early next day to abandon my carefully worked out strategy and go in search of Edna. I meant to tell her point-blank that I was in love with her, and let the whole world know about it as well. If she said no to me because I had not stolen public money and didn't have a Cadillac, well and good, I should go and bear it like a man. But I was determined not to carry on this surreptitious corner-corner love business one day longer. It would be wonderful, I thought, if I could present her to Max on his next visit here. He would be envious, I knew. Edna might not be a lawyer or sophisticated in the nail-varnish, eyebrow-shadow line like Eunice, but any man who passed Edna on the road and didn't look back must have a stiff neck. And as far as I was concerned she had just the right amount of education. I had nothing against professional women—in fact I liked them in their way—but if emancipation meant people like that other lady lawyer who came to sleep with illiterate

Chief Nanga for twenty-five pounds a time (as he confided to me next morning), then they could keep it.

During the fifteen-mile journey to Anata which took the greater part of forty minutes because of the corrugated laterite surface, I worked out what I was going to say. What was important was not so much what I said but that I should say it decisively and not like a mumbling schoolboy. If the answer wasn't yes it would be no; as they say, there are only two things you could do with yam—if you don't boil it, you roast it. Or perhaps I should preface my declaration with an account of what had been happening to me since we met last. Yes, she would certainly like to hear how her famous suitor came to me in the dark like Nicodemus and offered me two-fifty pounds. She would like that and if her greedy father was around it would make his mouth water into the bargain, and raise my standing in his eyes.

Then I remembered that last night as I thought about the offer I had been really angry again about it all. Not only about Max disgracing our party and yet having the face to charge me with idealism and naïvety, but I couldn't help feeling small at the inevitable comparison of the amounts offered to him and me. Not that it mattered; I would still have refused if it had been ten thousand. The real point surely was that Max's action had jeopardized our moral position, our ability to inspire that kind of terror which I had seen so clearly in Nanga's eyes despite all his grandiloquent bluff, and which in the end was our society's only hope of salvation.

I clearly saw Edna withdrawing hurriedly from the front room as I drove up. Women! No matter how beautiful they are they always try to be more—and usually fail; though in Edna's case she was great with face powder and the rest, and great without them.

Her younger brother was alone in the room. He stood up as I came in and said: "Good morning, sir."

"Good morning," I said. "Was it you brought me the letter?"

"Yes, sir."

"Thank you."

"Yes, sir."

"What is that you are reading?" He held out *The Sorrows of Satan,* one finger of his left hand still thrust into it to mark the page. I sat down.

"Is Edna in?"

"No, sir."

"What . . . ? Who did I see as I came up?"

He mumbled something confusedly.

"Go and call her!"

He stood where he was, looking on the floor.

"I said go and call her!" I shouted, rising to my feet. He made no move.

"All right," I said. "Edna!" I bawled out loud enough for the entire village to hear. She immediately came hurrying back.

What the hell is all this, or words to that effect, were on the tip of my tongue; but I wasn't allowed to say them. Edna wore a tightened-bow countenance you couldn't have thought possible on that face, and her tongue when she spoke (which was immediately) stung into me like the tail of a scorpion. I recoiled, tongue-tied.

"Some men have no shame. Can't you go and look for your own woman instead of sneaking around here? My father has told you to stop coming here, or have you come to pick up some gossip for your friend Mrs Nanga? A big fellow like you should be ashamed of gossiping like a woman. Errand boy, go and tell her I will marry Chief Nanga. Let her come and jump on my back if she can. As for you, why don't you go back to your prostitute-woman in Bori instead of wasting your time here? I have been respecting you for the sake of Chief Nanga, but if you make the mistake of coming here again I will tell you that my name is Edna Odo"—She turned to go, stopped again, called me "Mr Gossiper" in English and rushed away. . . .

"You better go before Dogo comes back. He says he will castrate you." This was from the boy, and it came after I had been standing rooted to the ground for I don't know how long. Dogo? Dogo? Who was he? I thought sluggishly like a slowed up action film. . . . Oh yes, Dogo the one-eyed bull. So he was guarding her. Well, well, good luck to them!

The first shock, the tightening in the throat passed very quickly, certainly by the time I had reversed my car and headed off. In retrospect my behaviour and reaction seemed to have broken all the rules in the book. I should have driven away in a daze, but I didn't. On the contrary my mind was as clear as daylight. The injustice of Edna's incoherent accusations most of which I couldn't even remotely relate to myself or anything I knew did not make me angry. Neither did the terrible thought that Chief Nanga had won the second round. What I felt was sadness—a sadness deep and cool like a well, into which my hopes had fallen; my twin hopes of a beautiful life with Edna and of a new era of cleanliness in the politics of our country.

A thought sneaked into my mind and told me it was futile now to try and go through with my political plans which in all honesty I should admit had always been a little nebulous— until Edna came along. She had been like a dust particle in the high atmosphere around which the water vapour of my thinking formed its globule of rain.

But I knew I would not heed that counsel, wherever it came from. The knowledge that Chief Nanga had won the first two rounds and, on the present showing, would win the third and last far from suggesting thoughts of surrender to my mind served to harden my resolution. What I had to accomplish became more than another squabble for political office; it rose suddenly to the heights of symbolic action, a shining, monumental gesture untainted by hopes of success or reward.

Chief Nanga moved swiftly and, as you would expect, ruthlessly. I was listening on my new portable transistor radio to the twelve o'clock news on the following Sunday morning. Those days I did not miss a single news bulletin. If I was likely not to be home at twelve, four, six or ten, I took my radio with me. It was a fine Japanese affair, no bigger than a camera, with an ear-piece which meant you could insulate yourself from the noisiest of surroundings. If I was driving somewhere I would park on the roadside until the news was over.

There were two reasons why I listened so avidly. In the first place news-thirst becomes a craving for every political activist, a kind of occupational disease. Secondly I wanted to keep a close watch on the antics of our national radio system which incidentally had not so far said a single word about the existence of our new party even though we had kept them fully informed of our activities. My Boniface and the others soon developed the same news-thirst, only they never did seem able to listen with their ears alone; they must pass their very loud comment at the same time, which was very distracting to me especially as their understanding of the news was sketchy and often fantastically distorted. So I began to cut them off by using the ear gadget.

"A-a, weting happen to the news?" asked puzzled Boniface the first time I played this trick.

"Radio done spoil," I said. "I just de hear am small for my ear now."

"We must go repairam," he said. "E no good make man de for darkness."

Two days later I had relented. I told them I had repaired the radio myself which impressed them a lot. The fact was I had begun to feel mean about cutting my faithful companions from their source of light. But also I had been missing Boniface's "Tiefman", "Foolis-man" and similar invective aimed at Chief Nanga and his ministerial colleagues whenever their names came up in the news—which was about every five seconds at normal peaceful times and much more frequently in these critical days.

But to return to the Sunday morning. I was listening in the outbuilding with the cynical amusement to which our radio station had now made me accustomed. I no longer had hopes of our latest story ever being used. I had thought that, with the telegram I had sent them on Friday, they would have been forced into giving us a brief mention. After all it was the first public appearance of a new party, the C.P.C., and the tacit support given my candidature by my village ought not to go unrecorded. True enough, my village was only one out of several in the constituency and their action might not affect the final verdict but what they had done was news by any definition of that word known to the civilized world.

But once more I listened in vain. Instead they announced Chief Nanga's inaugural campaign which had not even taken place! It was to happen on Monday week in Anata. Perhaps I should go and see it.

I was dully thinking about this when my father's name coming out of the radio stung me into full life. It was announced that Mr Hezekiah Samalu, chairman of P.O.P. in Urua, had been "ignominiously removed from his office for subversive, anti-party activities, according to an announcement received this morning from the P.O.P. Bureau of Investigation and Publicity".

I rushed into the main house and broke the news to my father who was then eating pounded yams and pepper soup at his small round table. He swallowed the ball of food in his hand and licked the soup from his fingers. I thought he was then going to say something. But he only shrugged his shoulders, drew out his lower lip in a gesture which said eloquently "Their own palaver, not mine", and continued eating.

The next day, however, the palaver came closer home. The local council Tax Assessment Officer brought him a reassessed figure based not only on his known pension of eighty-four pounds a year but on an alleged income of five hundred pounds derived from "business".

"What business?" everyone asked. But there was no time to explain. In the evening three local council policemen looking like "wee-wee" or marijuana smokers came to arrest him and in fact proceeded to manhandle him. I had to find twenty-four pounds fairly smartly; fortunately I had just enough C.P.C. money in the house to cover it. I threatened to take the matter up and the rascals laughed in my face. "Na only up you go take am?" asked their leader. "If I be you I go take am down too, when I done finish take am up. Turn you back make I see the nyarsh you go take fight Nanga."

"Foolis-man," said one of the others as they left.

The culmination came at the weekend when seven Public Works lorries arrived in the village and began to cart away the pipes they had deposited several months earlier for our projected Rural Water Scheme. This was the first indication we had that the Authorities did in fact hear of our little ceremony. Which was some consolation.

It is a sad truth of our nature that man becomes too easily brutalized by circumstance. The day after the tax incident I suddenly boiled over. I knew that Edna was still on the edge of my consciousness. I walked up stealthily from behind and pushed her down the precipice—out of my mind. I wrote to her.

Dear Edna, [I said] I wonder who ever put it into your beautiful empty head that I want to take you from your precious man. What on earth do you think I would want to do with a girl who has no more education than lower Elementary? By all means marry your ancient man and if you find that he is not up to it you can always steal away to his son's bed. Yours truly, Odili Samalu.

13

Two nights later we heard the sound of the Crier's gong. His message was unusual. In the past the Crier had summoned the village to a meeting to deliberate over a weighty question, or else to some accustomed communal labour. His business was to serve notice of something that was to happen. But this night he did something new: he announced a decision already taken. The elders and the councillors of Urua and the whole people, he said, had decided that in the present political fight raging in the land they should make it known that they knew one man and one man alone—Chief Nanga. Every man and every woman in Urua and every child and every adult would throw his or her paper for him on the day of election—as they had done in the past. If there was any other name called in the matter the elders and councillors of Urua had not heard it. He said this over and over again with minor changes in detail, like the omission of "every child" which I noticed particularly because it had struck me as odd in the first place. And I thought: if the whole people had taken the decision why were they now being told of it?

In the afternoon the radio, our national Crier, took up the message, amplified it and gave it in four languages including English. I listened to it, as I had listened to the rustic version, wearing my cynical smile. I couldn't say I blamed my village people for recoiling from the role of sacrificial ram. Why should they lose their chance of getting good, clean water, their share of the national cake? In fact they had adequate justification for their *volte-face* just two days later when the pipes returned. Or, at any rate, some of them returned. The rest apparently had been sent irrevocably to the neighbouring village of Ichida whose inhabitants had also been promised water but hadn't so far seen even one pipe. So the result of all my exertion had been to give Nanga one stone to kill two birds with.

When I came back with my newspapers the next day I was told that Councillor "Couple" had come to see my father with a promise that if he signed a certain document his recent tax levy would be refunded to him. The document merely sought to dissociate him from his son's lunatic activities; it also said that the so-called launching of C.P.C. in his premises was done without his knowledge and consent and concluded by affirming his implicit confidence in our great and God-fearing leader, Chief Nanga.

I could visualize my father reading it carefully with his now rarely used spectacles and, then putting his glasses aside, telling the fellow to carry his corpse off. And he must have run—so much so that he left the document behind.

"You made a serious mistake today," I told my father later that day.

"In your eyes have I ever done anything else in all my life?"

"I am talking about this paper you refused to sign."

He was silent for a while, then he said:

"You may be right. But our people have said that a man of worth never gets up to unsay what he said yesterday. I re-

ceived your friends in my house and I am not going to
deny it."

I thought to myself: You do not belong to this age, old
man. Men of worth nowadays simply forget what they said
yesterday. Then I realized that I had never really been close
enough to my father to understand him. I had built up a private picture of him from unconnected scraps of evidence. Was
this the same D.O.'s Interpreter who made a fortune out of the
ignorance of poor, illiterate villagers and squandered it on
drink and wives or had I got everything terribly, lopsidedly
wrong? Anyway, this was no time to begin a new assessment;
it was better left to the tax people.

"But one thing I must make clear," he said suddenly. "You
have brought this trouble into my compound so you should
carry it. From today whatever new tax they decide upon I will
pass the paper to you."

"That is a small matter," I said smiling, and I did mean
that it was a small matter.

I don't know what put it into my head to go to Chief Nanga's
inaugural campaign meeting. Did I want to learn some new
trick that I could put to use in my own campaign against him,
or was it naked curiosity—the kind that they say earned Mon-
key a bullet in the forehead? Whatever it was, I went. But I took
great pains to disguise myself first—with a hat and sun-glasses.
I thought of taking Boniface and the others, but decided they
were likely to attract attention and trouble. So I went alone.

I parked my car outside the Post Office and walked the
three hundred yards or so to the Court premises where the
meeting was already in progress. The time on my watch was
just a little after four. Even if I hadn't known my way in Anata
I could still have found the meeting easily enough. The sound
of drums and guns beckoned you on. And there were hundreds of other people going like me to the place. As I got
closer I could hear a brass band too—no doubt the Anata
Central School. I passed many villagers I knew and who
should remember one who was until recently a teacher at the

Grammar School, but they obviously had no clue who I was, which showed how good my disguise was. One such person was Josiah, the renegade trader. Those days he walked like a fowl drenched by rain. I came from behind and overtook him.

As soon as I turned into the Court premises my eyes caught Chief Nanga and his party sitting on a high platform solidly built from new timber. Of course I only noticed details like the timber when I had worked my way through the crowd to a closer position by ruthlessly widening every crack I saw in front of me and squeezing through, receiving abuses at my back. What I did see right away and what pulled me towards the dais was Edna sitting there on one side of Chief Nanga, much as she had done on that first day, like a convent girl. Mrs Nanga sat on the other side of her husband. All the other people on the platform so far were men, but there were still many empty chairs. When I had got to a point in the thick of the crowd from where I could observe the faces on the dais without attracting their attention I stopped.

The dais was surrounded by characters who looked as if they might be able to assist the police in various outstanding investigations. One-eyed Dogo was among them. Then of course there were the placard-carrying Nangavanga boys wearing silken, green, cowboy dresses. I noticed that none of the placards today had my name; I shouldn't have blabbed to Nanga about it. There were also about half a dozen policemen around—just in case, which was unlikely in this friendly crowd.

I was choking with the acrid smell of other people's sweat and wondered if the ceremony would ever begin.

Chief Nanga sat, smiling and cool in his white robes. His wife looking grandly matriarchal in a blue velvet "up-and-down" fanned herself with one of these delta-shaped Japanese fans, clearly too small and inadequate. Occasionally she lifted the neck of her blouse in front and blew left and right into her bosom. Edna just sat.

At last the ceremony seemed about to begin. Some party official wearing the green P.O.P. cap consulted with Chief Nanga who nodded several times, looking at his watch. Then the official grabbed the microphone and began to test it. His shrill voice amplified a hundredfold startled the crowd and then sent them laughing at their own fright. Something seemed to go wrong because the voice was superseded by one prolonged ear-tearing whistle. All other noises had stopped, and soon the high-pitched whistle stopped too. The man counted one to ten and the crowd laughed again. Then he announced that he was the M.C. He said the man before us needed no introduction (hell, I thought, not again!)—"he was no other than the great Honourable Minister Chief Doctor (in advance) M. A. Nanga."

I did not listen to the many virtues of Chief Nanga as enumerated by this M.C., partly because I knew them very well already but also because the fellow having presumably lost his own eardrums long ago was showing no respect at all to ours . . . I put my hands over the ears to break the sharp-pointed assault. And to pass the time while waiting for Nanga's speech I began to exercise my fancy. What would happen if I were to push my way to the front and up the palm-leaf-festooned dais, wrench the microphone from the greasy hands of that blabbing buffoon and tell the whole people—this vast contemptible crowd—that the great man they had come to hear with their drums and dancing was an Honourable Thief. But of course they knew that already. No single man and woman there that afternoon was stranger to that news—not even the innocent-looking convent girl on the dais. And because they all knew, if I were to march up to the dais now and announce it they would simply laugh at me and say: What a fool! Whose son is he? Was he not here when white men were eating; what did he do about it? Where was he when Chief Nanga fought and drove the white men away? Why is he envious now that the warrior is eating the reward of his courage? If he was Chief Nanga, would he not do much worse?

These questions would not, of course, be spread out into so many words; more likely they would be compressed into a few sharp blows to the head. . . .

As my mind dozed lazily on these fanciful thoughts I saw Josiah, the outlawed trader, mount the few steps to the dais and whisper to Chief Nanga who sprang up immediately searching the crowd. Josiah then turned round and pointed in my direction. I turned sharply at the same time and began to push blindly through the crowd, panic-stricken, appearing to make no progress whatever. Then I heard the loudspeakers call out to the crowd to stop that man wearing a hat and dark glasses. I took off the hat. For a brief moment nothing happened and I struggled through a few more bodies. Then some tentative hands tried to stop me from behind but I shook them off and continued to push and shove.

"I said stop that thief trying to run away!" screamed the loudspeaker. The hands gained a little resolution and one vaguely-seen body stood firmly in my way. But I was not running any more then. I wanted to know who called me a thief. So I turned round and was pushed forward from three sides to the foot of the dais.

"Odili the great," saluted Chief Nanga. Then he took the microphone and said: "My people, this is the boy who wants to take my seat." The announcement was greeted by a wild uproar, compounded of disbelief, shock and contemptuous laughter. "Come up here," said Nanga. "They want to see you." I was pushed up the steps to the dais. As I went up I noticed that Edna had covered her face with both hands.

"My people," said Nanga again. "This is the boy who is thrusting his finger into my eye. He came to my house in Bori, ate my food, drank my water and my wine and instead of saying thank you to me he set about plotting how to drive me out and take over my house." The crowd roared again. My panic had now left me entirely and in its place I found a rock-cold fearlessness that I had never before felt in my heart. I watched Nanga, microphone in one hand, reeling about the dais in drunken jubilation. I seemed to see him from a superior, impregnable position.

"I hear some people asking who is he: I will tell you. He was once my pupil. I taught him ABC and I called him to my house to arrange for him to go to England. Yes, I take the blame; he did not just smell his hand one morning and go to my house—I called him. Anyone who wants to may blame me." There were louder cries of shock at such an unspeakable betrayal. "He even tried to take a girl on whose head I had put the full bride-price and many other expenses—and who according to our custom is my wife—this girl here. . . ." He went over to Edna and roughly pulled her hands away from her face. "He tried to take this girl who is covering her face for shame. Fortunately my wife caught him and told me." He turned aside from the crowd to me. "Odili the great! So you have come to seek me out again. You are very brave; or have you come to seek Edna, eh? That's it. Come to the microphone and tell my people why you came; they are listening . . ." He thrust the microphone into my face.

"I came to tell your people that you are a liar and . . ." He pulled the microphone away smartly, set it down, walked up to me and slapped my face. Immediately hands seized my arms, but I am happy that he got one fairly good kick from me. He slapped me again and again. Edna rushed forward crying and tried to get between us but he pushed her aside so violently that she landed on her buttocks on the wooden platform. The roar of the crowd was now like a thick forest all around. By this time blows were falling as fast as rain on my head and body until something heavier than the rest seemed to split my skull. The last thing I remembered was seeing all the policemen turn round and walk quietly away.

The events of the next four weeks or so have become so widely known in the world at large that there would be little point in my relating them in any detail here. And in any case, while those events were happening I was having a few private problems of my own. My cracked cranium took a little time to mend—to say nothing of the broken arm and countless severe bruises one of which all but turned me into a kind of genealogical cul-de-sac.

I remember the first time I woke up in the hospital and felt my head turbanned like an Alhaji. Everything seemed unreal and larger than life and I was sure I was dreaming. In the dream I saw Edna and my father and Mama standing around my bed. I also saw, through a gap in the screen, two policemen. But the only thing that was immediate and in focus was that pressure trapped inside the head pounding away in a panic effort to escape. I tried to feel my turban but the pain followed my thought to the arm—and I went off again. The next time I looked around me my father and Mama and the policemen were still there, and they looked more solid than the last time. Edna had vanished. Perhaps her figure had been planted there in the first place by my fevered fancy. I wondered—in a dull, faraway manner—what the police were doing beside my bed. But I did not wonder too much nor too long. Every other single thing was strange anyway and two policemen (or four when they were changing guards) didn't make much difference. (Perhaps it was their way of making amends for their desertion when I had needed them.) But one morning I woke up to find they had disappeared. "Where are they?" I asked the nurse who brought my medicine.

"They done go."

"But why?"

"You de ask why, instead to thank God that they done withdraw your case?"

My case? I tried hard to remember but couldn't and gave up. My father should be coming any minute now and he would know. But when he came and I asked him he refused to tell, saying I should get better first. But I kept at him until he said yes, I had been under arrest for being found in possession of dangerous weapons.

"Found, where? Who found me?"

"In your car. They said five matchets were found in your car and two double-barrelled guns. Anyway they have now withdrawn the case."

My thoughts were slowly coming into focus. "What day is the election?"

"I don't know."

"Say you won't tell me, but not that you don't know," I said petulantly. "Could I have my radio?"

"Not yet; the doctor says you are to rest."

The next day I asked again and if only to save himself from my pestering importunity he said yes, the thugs had ransacked my car, overturned it and set it on fire; then after I had been brought to hospital I was placed under arrest ostensibly for having weapons in my car but really to prevent me from signing my nomination paper.

"Nomination paper? But I have already signed it," I said.

"No, that first one never reached the Electoral Officer. It was seized by thugs from your people on their way to the Electoral Office . . ."

I tried to sit up but he pressed me back; not that I could have made it, anyway.

"Now I have told you. Don't ask me any more questions, do you hear me? Even in this hospital you cannot say who is a friend and who an enemy. That is why I am here so much." He said this quietly and with a backward glance. "Max came here in person with a new nomination paper for you but they turned him back."

"I see."

It was in fact election day as we spoke. My father found it easy to conceal the fact from me because they had put me in a special isolated ward. That same night Max was killed in Abaga but I didn't hear of it either, until two days after; and then I wept all day that day, and the pressure inside my head returned and I hoped I would die, but the doctor put me to sleep.

As I got the story later from Joe, the trade-unionist, Max had been informed by our party intelligence that Chief Koko's resourceful wife was leading the Women's Wing of the P.O.P. in an operation that one might describe as breastfeeding the ballot, i.e. smuggling into the polling booths wads of ballot paper concealed in their brassières. Max immediately investigated. But as soon as he alighted from his car, one of Chief Koko's jeeps swept up from behind, knocked him over and killed him on the spot.

The police, most of whom turned out to be disguised party thugs, performed half-hearted motions to arrest the driver of the jeep but Chief S. I. Koko came forward and told them not to worry; he would handle the matter himself. Eunice had been missed by a few inches when Max had been felled. She stood like a stone figure, I was told, for some minutes more. Then she opened her handbag as if to take out a handkerchief, took out a pistol instead and fired two bullets into Chief Koko's chest. Only then did she fall down on Max's body and begin to weep like a woman; and then the policemen seized her and dragged her away. A very strange girl, people said.

The fighting which broke out that night between Max's bodyguard and Chief Koko's thugs in Abaga struck a match and lit the tinder of discontent in the land. Nearer home in Anata Chief Nanga, having been elected unopposed, tried to disband his private army, if only to save himself their keep; but some of them refused to be disbanded and staged a minor battle in which Dogo (the one-eyed bodyguard) lost an ear. Then they went on a rampage, sacking one market after another in the district, seizing women's wares and beating up people. My father's youngest wife lost her entire stock of dried fish in our village market during one of their raids and got a swollen face instead. Other election thugs in different parts of the country hearing of the successes of Chief Nanga's people quickly formed their own bands of marauders. And so a minor reign of terror began.

Meanwhile the Prime Minister had appointed Chief Nanga and the rest of the old Cabinet back to office and announced over the radio that he intended to govern and stamp out subversion and thuggery without quarter or mercy. He assured foreign investors that their money was safe in the country, that his government stood "as firm as the Rock of Gibraltar" by its open-door economic policy. "This country," he said, "has never been more united or more stable than it is today." He nominated Chief Koko's widow to the Senate and from there made her Minister for Women's Affairs, intending to quiet the powerful guild of Bori market women who had become restive.

Some political commentators have said that it was the supreme cynicism of these transactions that inflamed the people and brought down the Government. That is sheer poppycock.

The people themselves, as we have seen, had become even more cynical than their leaders and were apathetic into the bargain. "Let them eat," was the people's opinion, "after all when white men used to do all the eating did we commit suicide?" Of course not. And where is the all-powerful white man today? He came, he ate and he went. But we are still around. The important thing then is to stay alive; if you do you will outlive your present annoyance. The great thing, as the old people have told us, is reminiscence; and only those who survive can have it. Besides, if you survive, who knows? it may be your turn to eat tomorrow. Your son may bring home your share.

No, the people had nothing to do with the fall of our Government. What happened was simply that unruly mobs and private armies having tasted blood and power during the election had got out of hand and ruined their masters and employers. And they had no public reason whatever for doing it. Let's make no mistake about that.

One day just before I left hospital Edna came to see me. We looked at each other without speaking. What could I say about that letter in which I had called her an uneducated girl and said many other crude things besides? But attack, they say, is the best defence. So I attacked. "Congratulations," I said. "I will never contest his seat again." I smiled falsely. She said nothing, just stood where she was, staring at me with those round, rock-melting eyes. "I am terribly sorry, Edna," I said. "I have behaved like an animal . . . I will always remember that in all that crowd you were the only one who tried to help me." My eyes clouded. "Don't cry," I said when I looked at her again and found my tears running down her face. "Please, my love, don't. Come and sit here." And SHE DID.

"Edna, I don't know . . . I feel like a beast . . . believe me . . . about that letter . . . I was so unhappy . . . you can't imagine how miserable I was. Will you ever forgive me?"

"Forgive you? For what? Everything you said in it is true."

"Oh please don't talk like that, Edna. I know how you must feel. But please I didn't mean to . . . you know. I was so confused and I didn't want to . . . I didn't want you to go and marry that idiot. That was why . . . To God . . ." I tried instinctively to seal the oath by touching my lips and pointing to the sky with my swearing finger, forgetting momentarily in my confusion that my right arm was in plaster. I was reminded soon enough, and changed to my left finger which felt odd.

"Marry him? To be frank with you I did not want to marry him . . . All the girls in the college were laughing at me . . . It was only my father . . . I don't claim to know book but at least . . ."

"Oh please, Edna――――"

". . . at least I thank God that I am better than some people with all their minister and everything. He is no better than any bush, jaguda man, with all his money. And what you said, about his wife's jealousy――――"

"Wait a bit," I said, something having clicked inside my head and told me to pay some attention to what the other party was saying. "Wait a bit. Are we talking about my first letter or the second?"

"Second? Which second letter? Did you write two?"

"Yes, after I came to see you," I said and then said to myself: Don't let up, man! Attack and cover your defences. "Yes, when I came to see you and you made me so miserable . . . I wrote; you mean you didn't get it?"

"No, I did not. After you came to see me? . . . It must be one of those the postmaster handed over to him."

"Postmaster? I don't understand."

"Oh, you didn't hear? The postmaster and the man are like this." She dovetailed her fingers. "He was passing all my letters to him."

"No! What a beast!"

"Have you ever seen a thing like that? It was only God that saved me from his hands."

"God and Odili."

"Yes, and Odili . . . What did you say in it?"

"In what? Oh the letter . . . Yes, well, the usual things."

"Tell me."

"I will, later. Let's talk about new things now, about our future plans." After a short silence of contemplation on this unbelievable piece of good fortune I said somewhat lightheartedly: "A whole Cabinet Minister prying into a little girl's love-letters!"

"Have you ever seen such bad luck!" said Edna, and then something seemed to dawn on her and she asked: "But who is a little girl?"

I smiled and squeezed her hand, then pursued my own thoughts aloud.

"The inquisitive eye will only blind its own sight," I pronounced. "A man who insists on peeping into his neighbour's bedroom knowing a woman to be there is only punishing himself."

It was then Edna's turn to squeeze my good hand.

We heard my father's voice greeting the nurse in the main ward and Edna quickly got up from my bed and sat on a chair.

"Ah, my daughter!" he said. "You have kept away so long. I began to think I had frightened you away."

"No, sir," she said embarrassed.

"Frightened her away? How?"

"I told her I was going to marry her for one of my sons that day she spent a whole night with us here . . ."

"So it wasn't a dream?"

"What dream?"

"Never mind, father. What I mean is you should marry her for this son here."

"That remains to be seen."

After my illness my father, some of his close relatives and I went with a big pot of palm-wine to Edna's father to start a "conversation". The first few visits we made no headway at all. Our host simply refused to believe that he had lost a Chief and Minister as son-in-law and must now settle for this crazy boy who had bought a tortoise and called it a car. But the Army obliged us by staging a coup at that point and locking up every member of the Government. The rampaging bands of election thugs had caused so much unrest and dislocation that our young Army officers seized the opportunity to take over. We were told Nanga was arrested trying to escape by canoe dressed like a fisherman.

Thereafter we made rapid progress with Edna's father who, no doubt, saw me then as a bird in hand. He told us that Chief Nanga had paid a bride-price of one hundred and fifty pounds for his daughter and another one hundred pounds on her education and other incidentals. Was that all? I thought.

"Our custom," said my father firmly, "is to return the bride-price—finish. Other bits and pieces must be the man's loss. Is that not the custom?" Our party said yes, that was the custom.

As indeed it was. But I was not interested in legalistic-traditional arguments just now, especially when they were calculated to delay things (a coup might be followed by a counter coup and then where would we be?); and anyway I did not want to go through life thinking that I owed Chief Nanga money spent on my wife's education. So I agreed—to my people's astonishment—to pay everything. "Let us go outside and whisper together," said my scandalized relations. I said a flat no and they shrugged their acquiescence, astonished at my firmness—and pleased, because we admire firmness.

I had already decided privately to borrow the money from C.P.C. funds still in my hands. They were not likely to be needed soon, especially as the military regime had just abolished all political parties in the country and announced they would remain abolished "until the situation became stabilized once again". They had at the same time announced the impending trial of all public servants who had enriched themselves by defrauding the state. The figure involved was said to be in the order of fifteen million pounds.

But their most touching gesture as far as I was concerned was to release Eunice from jail and pronounce Max a Hero of the Revolution. (For I must point out that my severe criticism of his one fatal error notwithstanding, Max was indeed a hero and martyr; and I propose to found a school—a new type of school, I hasten to add—in my village to his memory.) What I found distasteful however was the sudden, unashamed change of front among the very people who had stood by and watched him die.

Overnight everyone began to shake their heads at the excesses of the last regime, at its graft, oppression and corrupt government: newspapers, the radio, the hitherto silent intellectuals and civil servants—everybody said what a terrible lot; and it became public opinion the next morning. And these were the same people that only the other day had owned a thousand names of adulation, whom praise-singers followed with song and talking-drum wherever they went. Chief Koko in particular became a thief and a murderer, while the people who had led him on—in my opinion the real culprits—took the legendary bath of the Hornbill and donned innocence.

"Koko has taken enough for the owner to see," said my father to me. It was the day I had gone to visit Eunice and was telling him on my return how the girl had showed no interest in anything—including whether she stayed in jail or out of it. My father's words struck me because they were the very same words the villagers of Anata had spoken of Josiah, the abominated trader. Only in their case the words had meaning. The owner was the village, and the village had a mind; it could say no to sacrilege. But in the affairs of the nation there was no owner, the laws of the village became powerless. Max was avenged not by the people's collective will but by one solitary woman who loved him. Had his spirit waited for the people to demand redress it would have been waiting still, in the rain and out in the sun. But he was lucky. And I don't mean it to shock or to sound clever. For I do honestly believe that in the fat-dripping, gummy, eat-and-let-eat regime just ended—a regime which inspired the common saying that a man could only be sure of what he had put away safely in his gut or, in language ever more suited to the times: "you chop, me self I chop, palaver finish"; a regime in which you saw a fellow cursed in the morning for stealing a blind man's stick and later in the evening saw him again mounting the altar of the new shrine in the presence of all the people to whisper into the ear of the chief celebrant—in such a regime, I say, you died a good death if your life had inspired someone to come forward and shoot your murderer in the chest—without asking to be paid.